"GADS, YOU'RE FULL OF YOURSELF, AREN'T YOU?"

Link shrugged. "What can I say? People want to work for me because they want to see how I work. How my mind works," he said more precisely.

"And how does your mind work?" Annie asked.

"I don't think you want to know," he said, his gaze traveling down the front of her.

"Hmm." She frowned and leaned forward to brush a lock of hair behind his ear.

He wasn't sure if she didn't understand what he meant, or if she didn't want to understand. He knew, with her this close, he couldn't resist the temptation. Reaching forward, he snagged her by the waist and pulled her to him.

"Link!" she squealed. Before she could react, he had her seated facing him, her shorts-clad bottom resting on his thighs and her face level with his.

"What?" he asked, leaning forward to brush a kiss over her cheek.

"This isn't a good idea," she said, but didn't move.

"I think it's a very good idea," he murmured, and teased her with a kiss on her other cheek.

"We shouldn't—"

She didn't finish. Perhaps because he'd silenced her words by touching his lips to hers.

He kissed Annie with a longing he hadn't known for years. . . .

WHAT ARE *LOVESWEPT* ROMANCES?

They are stories of true romance and touching emotion. We believe those two very important ingredients are constants in our highly sensual and very believable stories in the LOVE-SWEPT line. Our goal is to give you, the reader, stories of consistently high quality that may sometimes make you laugh, sometimes make you cry, but are always fresh and creative and contain many delightful surprises within their pages.

Most romance fans read an enormous number of books. Those they truly love, they keep. Others may be traded with friends and soon forgotten. We hope that each LOVESWEPT romance will be a treasure—a "keeper." We will always try to publish

LOVE STORIES YOU'LL NEVER FORGET
BY AUTHORS YOU'LL ALWAYS REMEMBER

The Editors

CHASE
THE
DREAM

MARIS
SOULE

BANTAM BOOKS
NEW YORK · TORONTO · LONDON · SYDNEY · AUCKLAND

CHASE THE DREAM

A Bantam Book / February 1998

ISBN 0-553-44596-0

Published simultaneously in the United States and Canada

Bantam Books are published by Bantam Books, a division of Bantam Dou-
bleday Dell Publishing Group, Inc. Its trademark, consisting of the words
"Bantam Books" and the portrayal of a rooster, is Registered in U.S. Patent
and Trademark Office and in other countries. Marca Registrada. Bantam
Books, 1540 Broadway, New York, New York 10036.

PRINTED IN THE UNITED STATES OF AMERICA

OPM   10 9 8 7 6 5 4 3 2 1

My thanks to Lisa Cardle. She taught
Annie Marsden everything she needed
to know.

ONE

The clouds slipped away from the moon, and a silvery white light spilled across the gravestones, illuminating one with ghostly distinction. She headed for it, totally unaware of the shadowy figure behind her. Suddenly a chill ran down her spine, and . . .

—The Long Silence

Annie heard a sound.

Half groan and half cry, it jolted her out of the story and into action. The book went facedown on the comforter, and she scooted off the daybed. The moment her feet hit the plush carpeting, she was on the move.

She took the steps up the curving staircase two at a time. Above her, she heard another groan, followed by words she couldn't make out. As soon as she reached the landing, Annie dashed for the great room, thankful that she'd left on a light, albeit dimmed.

She could see him on the hospital bed that had been

brought into the house specifically for him. He was thrashing and twisting under a lightweight sheet and blanket, all the while making sounds that were a mixture of words and moans. If he kept on moving around like that, at best he was going to bruise his arms, and at worst he was going to pull out the stitches the doctors had so carefully put in.

"Can't," she heard him shout, and he pulled on the blanket, dragging it up off the cast on his right leg. She closed the distance between them.

"Dr. Sheffield," she called, hoping she didn't startle him. "Link," she added, when she remembered he'd told her to call him that.

"No, don't go," he cried out, lifting his left arm toward her.

Annie was afraid he was going to hit his elbow against the bed's side railing. "Link," she repeated, grabbing him by the wrist and holding his arm away from the metal. "It's all right."

At her touch, his eyes opened, but she could read the confusion. "It's me," she said quickly. "Annie. Annie Marsden. Your nurse."

He still looked bewildered, and she went on. "I got here this afternoon. Remember? Your uncle set it up. I'm going to be living here, in your house. Staying with you until your wounds are healed and you can get along on your own. You've been in the hospital. There was an accident. An explosion in your lab."

Annie knew she was talking too fast, but her words were having the desired effect. In the depths of his dark

brown eyes, she saw the recognition. He was remembering.

She eased his arm back onto the bed and touched his
forehead above the bandage on his temple. Gently, she
brushed a lock of his rumpled brown hair back into place.

Immediately he frowned, pulling his head to the side.
"Don't."

"Sorry." She drew her hand back. "Are you all right?"

"No, I'm not all right. You wouldn't be here, would
you, if I were all right?"

"No, I guess not." She smiled. "Okay, then. Are you
in any pain? Do you need a pain pill?"

"No."

His answer was firm, but considering the way he'd
been groaning when she came into the room, she had her
doubts that it was honest. "It's all right, you know. According to the doctor's notes, you can have pain medication as often as you need it."

"I said, I don't want a pain pill." He ground out the
words.

"Okay." She got the message. "If you want to play the
macho, 'no pain, no gain' bit, that's fine with me." He
mumbled something she didn't understand, and she
fought another smile. "Are you always going to be this
friendly?"

"I wasn't aware that I had to be friendly." He shifted
position, moving away from her. "I just don't like to be
fussed over."

"Then I won't fuss over you. I'm here to help you."

He grunted, looking away, and she grinned. "You
know, being grumpy isn't going to help anything."

"I'm not being grumpy."

"Right." From the start, Link Sheffield, Ph.D., had been a grump. His first words to her had been, "Go home. I don't need you." Which was ridiculous. In her opinion, the man shouldn't even be out of the hospital. He looked like a war casualty, his body bruised and battered and covered with bandages, and his right leg encased in a cast from midthigh to his toes.

Not that she found his appearance grotesque or repulsive. He had beautiful dark brown eyes and his features reminded her a little of Christian Slater's. Even his body build did. Though not overly muscular, Link had a lean masculinity she found very appealing. His uncle, Ron Sheffield, who had met her at the door earlier that day and introduced her to his nephew, had the same lean build and good looks.

Link's uncle was in his late fifties and very concerned about his nephew. Right away he'd warned her that Link wasn't in a good mood. That had been an understatement, as far as Annie was concerned. Link had grumbled and groused all the time his uncle was there, all through supper, and all through the evening. Annie had no doubts that she was going to have her hands full for the next week or two. Even the instructions and chart the doctor had sent along with various medications and supplies indicated that Link wouldn't be an easy patient. But she'd dealt with difficult patients before, and the pay for this job was going to be higher than she normally got. With college debts still hanging over her head, every penny counted.

Link glanced back at her, his gaze dropping to her nightshirt. "You were in bed?"

"Reading," she said, also looking down at her nightshirt. It was cotton and loose-fitting, revealing little more of her body than her street clothes. She did notice her nipples were hard and making quite obvious puckers in the cotton, but with her small breasts, that wasn't anything shocking. If anything about her attire was going to shock him, she had a feeling it was the hot pink color and wild zodiac design. She'd never bought into the idea of quiet pastels for sleeping. "I like bright colors," she said, and moved to the end of the bed.

"Obviously." He pushed one of the buttons on the side panel that controlled the bed, raising his head slightly so he could watch as she pulled the blanket up off his legs.

She felt his gaze on her, but ignored him. First she turned up the light, then she checked the toes poking out from his cast, giving his big toe a squeeze. Color was good, she noted, temperature normal. However, according to the doctor's instructions, the leg was to be kept elevated, and right now it was nearly flat on the bed. The pillows that should have been under it were pushed to the side, and one by one, she slid them back under his cast.

"You were doing a lot of thrashing around," she said, grabbing the last pillow and lifting his leg even higher. "Were you trying to get away from something?"

"No. Dammit, what are you doing?"

"I'm trying to get your leg up high enough so it doesn't swell."

"Well, you don't have to jerk it around like that."

"I wasn't jerking it around. I was—" She stopped herself. Letting him irritate her wasn't going to help the situation. And maybe she had been a little rougher than she'd realized. She forced a smile and softened her tone. "I apologize. I will try to be more careful in the future."

"Yeah, right."

She shook her head; he even groused over an apology. Keeping the smile in place, she walked back to his side. "Considering how much you were moving around, I should also look at the dressing on your stomach."

"So look."

He eased the bed back to a level position, and she pulled the covers down far enough to expose his pajama top and the surgical dressing on his right side. He'd been lucky that the shard of glass that had pierced his skin hadn't severed any major blood vessels, but according to his medical chart, the gash was deep and stitches now held a portion of his small intestine together.

She checked for signs of blood or discoloration. In the morning, the dressing would need to be changed. For now, she simply had to watch for bleeding or signs of infection. Seeing neither, she pulled the covers back up. "Well, I guess you're none the worst for your nightmare. Do you want to talk about it?"

"Talk about it?" Again, he frowned. "About my dream?"

"Sometimes it helps. Puts things in focus."

"I don't need to put 'things' in focus."

"Suit yourself." She grinned. "Well, since you don't want any fussing, and it doesn't look like you did any damage to those sutures, I think I'll go back to my book. That is, unless there's something else you need."

Annie Marsden's efficiency and politeness irritated Link. He liked it better when she snapped at him, when he knew he was upsetting her. Dammit all, he didn't want this woman in his house. Long ago, he'd sworn he would never again be dependent on a woman. Women, he'd learned, couldn't be relied on. They left when you needed them. Took off, never to be seen again.

Annie started to walk away, and he grimaced. Like it or not, he did need her. He needed her right now. "Wait," he said, stopping her. She turned and faced him. "I need to pee," he said, knowing he shouldn't be embarrassed by the fact. After all, it was a normal human function. Nevertheless, he felt uncomfortable with the request.

Maybe it would be easier if she looked more like a nurse. But nurses didn't go around barefoot, wearing hot pink nightshirts with psychedelic fish on the front, nightshirts that barely reached their knees and showed off shapely legs. They didn't look at you with big blue eyes that delved into your soul and made you forget you didn't need a woman. Nor did they have short brown hair that looked like it had been styled with an eggbeater and begged to be touched. Nurses were nondescript androids who poked and prodded and asked stupid questions, like "How are we feeling today?"

He was feeling rotten.

And his bladder was full.

"I'll get something," she said with a knowing smile.

He stared at the ceiling and listened to her go into the

bathroom. He knew he should have stayed in the hospital a few more days, but with his uncle preparing to leave the country for two months, it was make the move now or end up in a nursing home until he was on his feet.

Just the idea of being cooped up in one of those institutions made Link blanch. Maybe they were fine once you were old, but he was only thirty-three. No way were they putting him in a nursing home.

"I know you have a lot of bruises," Annie said, coming back to his side, "so getting you in position so you can do this may be a little uncomfortable."

Link had a feeling it wasn't his bruises that were going to cause him discomfort. "So, do you nurses all get a thrill out of doing this?"

She lifted her eyebrows as she lowered the side railing. "Hardly."

He wondered. "You probably all gather in the break room and compare sizes."

She laughed as she pushed back the blanket and sheet, exposing his printed boxer shorts. "You guys and your preoccupation with size. Trust me, we couldn't care less."

"Sure." He focused on the two fish crossing the front of her nightshirt and wondered if she was wearing anything underneath it. From the way her nipples were poking at the bright pink cotton, he had a feeling she wasn't. And though she certainly didn't have a bustline to brag about, he found the thought of her naked exciting.

Which was a mistake. It was either that or her hand touching his hip that brought on the response, but he could feel himself growing hard. She was not only going to know his size, he was going to make taking a pee impossible.

"Relax," she said softly.

Easier said than done, he thought.

"Can you handle it yourself?" she asked. "Or do you want me to help?"

He grunted at the innuendo and glanced down at the pee pot she had in position. "I'll handle it."

As he relieved himself, he tried to remember the last time he'd been with a woman. For a while after Marian walked out on him, he'd bounced from bed to bed. That had been years ago, when he'd felt a need to prove himself. Somewhere along the way maturity had taken over, along with a driving desire to make enough money to prove Marian had been wrong to leave him. Lately he'd been so immersed in perfecting a fuel cell for an electric car that he hadn't had time for a woman. It had to have been months since he'd been with one, and then it hadn't been in this position.

He sighed and finished.

She took the bowl from him and pulled the covers back up, then stepped away from the bed. "I'll take care of this."

He watched her until she was out of sight, then he closed his eyes. This wasn't going to work, he told himself. Problem was, he couldn't think of an alternative. Necessity might be the mother of all inventions, but the time to think about inventing a robot nurse was not while you were lying flat on your back in a hospital bed. At least, it wasn't going to solve his present problem.

In the bathroom Annie washed her hands and dried

them, then glanced into the mirror and grinned. She had a feeling Link Sheffield, when he wasn't all cut up and bruised, was a very good-looking man and probably turned many a woman's head. She wondered how many of those women had seen him as she'd just seen him. She knew it had been difficult for him to ask for her help. Men were funny that way. Even her brother got embarrassed when she reminded him that she'd changed his diapers.

Ah, yes, men and their egos. They were always trying to prove something. Who was stronger, faster . . . bigger? From what she'd seen, Link Sheffield didn't have anything to be ashamed of.

Laughing at the direction her thoughts had headed, Annie started back to the great room. But she paused before returning to Link's side. Paused and stared.

In front of her was one of the most spectacular views she'd ever seen. Through ceiling-to-floor windows was a panoramic view of the San Francisco Bay Area, and though the sky was dark, the city below sparkled with lights, both stationary and moving.

She could see where the Nimitz Freeway cut through Oakland and turned onto the Bay Bridge, the cars on it rushing to or from San Francisco. Farther on, on the other side of the bay and the San Francisco skyline, she could see the lights of the Golden Gate Bridge and the point where it ran into Marin County. Even the water was replete with lights, some on ships, others acting as warnings of shallow depths.

None of the windows of her two-bedroom tract house in Lafayette had a view like this, but then her house wasn't built on the side of the Oakland-Berkeley foothills and didn't cost over a million dollars. Knowing her patient had money didn't excuse his grumpiness, but it was certainly going to make her living accommodations for the next two weeks more enjoyable. Even her bedroom, one flight down, had a view similar to the one she was looking at. This would be an experience she would remember for years.

Simply parking in Link's carport that looked out onto his roof and taking an elevator down to the first floor of his home had been an experience. She'd never been inside a house built into a hill, or one where street level was above the living quarters. Once inside, she had forced herself not to gawk, but it hadn't been easy.

On the first floor was the kitchen, formal dining room, bathroom, laundry room, and the great room, which took up the front half of the house. Everything was carpeted in muted colors; the furnishings were masculine in design and crafted of solid wood, primarily oak; and the accents were appropriately colorful, blues and greens dominating. Annie had a feeling some decorator had made a bundle from this assignment.

In the great room, in addition to the hospital bed that had been recently introduced, there were two easy chairs, a sofa, two end tables, and the biggest entertainment center she'd ever seen. The television screen was almost theater size.

A curved staircase led down to the lowest level, where Link's uncle had shown her the three bedrooms, Link's being the largest. One of the smaller rooms, the one with the daybed, had been assigned to her. Not that she minded. From her brief time on that bed, she'd found it comfortable, and the room wasn't much smaller than the master bedroom at her house.

"Are you going to just stand there, or are you going to do something?" Link asked from his bed, and she looked away from the window.

"I was admiring your view," she said, walking back to his side. "It's quite spectacular."

"I suppose."

"My living room looks out on a postage-size backyard and a rotting wooden fence." She straightened the covers around his shoulders.

"You're fussing again."

She stopped and shook her head. "And you're grumbling again."

"Do you always talk back to your patients?"

"Usually."

"You can be replaced, you know."

"I'll make the call, if you'd like."

"Ready to bail out?"

"You're the one making the threats, not me."

"Just because I can't get out of this bed—"

"Doesn't give you the right to be rude."

He glared at her, his eyes boring into hers, but she didn't look away. If he wanted a nursemaid who would jump at every order he gave, she wasn't the one for him, and they would both be a lot better off if they got that straight right away, even if it meant her losing this job.

He looked away first. "I don't like being in this position."

"I can't imagine anyone liking it," she said.

He turned back to her. "How old are you?"

"Twenty-seven."

"You don't look that old."

She smiled. "Well, I am."

"I didn't see any rings. Do I assume you're single?"

"Again."

"Again?"

"Divorce was final six years ago."

"You left him?"

"We parted by mutual agreement."

Link knew what that meant. Either she'd gotten tired of playing wife or things had gotten rough. No wonder marriage ceremonies were leaving out the "For better or worse, through thick and thin" part. Those vows didn't mean anything anymore.

"Anything else you want to know?" She ran a hand through her hair, doing nothing to tame its wild look.

"Hey, I'm trying to be friendly." He forced a smile. "I thought that was what you wanted."

"Okay. Fair enough. Here goes. Annie Marsden, in fifty words or less. I'm one of three children—have an older sister and a younger brother. Both parents still living. Married at eighteen and filed for divorce at twenty-one. Nursing degree from Merritt College, live in Lafayette, in a house that's probably not much bigger than this room. I've been doing private nursing for three years now. I like cats, reading mysteries, and solving cryptograms. I don't like rude people."

"Meaning me."

"Meaning anyone who's rude." She pulled the side rail back up. "May I ask you a question?"

"Maybe."

"Meaning maybe you'll answer me, or maybe you won't." She grinned. "Okay. When you're working with something that can blow up, why don't you take precautions? You could have been killed."

"What I was working on shouldn't have blown up."

"And that's why you're lying on this bed with multiple fractures to your leg, sutures in your small intestine, and looking like you just came off the war zone."

"The fuel cell was working fine," he insisted. "There was no reason for it to blow up."

She nodded, and he knew she didn't believe him.

"We're not talking about a gasoline fuel cell," he said. "This was a fuel cell for an electric car."

"I thought electric cars used electricity."

"They're powered by some manner of energy. Most of the EVs—electric vehicles—on the road right now are being powered by hydride batteries or lead-acid batteries, but they're not efficient enough. The batteries are too heavy, the mileage too limited. But soon EVs will be powered by lightweight lithium batteries or hydrogen fuel cells. It's the hydrogen fuel cell that I've been working on. With those, you'll be able to pull into a station and fill up with hydrogen, just like you fill up with gas now. Then, as you're driving along, the fuel cell will make the electricity necessary to run the car from the hydrogen mixing with the oxygen in the air, and the only waste product will be water."

"Now that would be interesting to see."

"All you have to do is go up to Vancouver, British Columbia." This wasn't some pipe dream of the future.

"There's a bus there running daily on exactly what I described."

She cocked her head, clearly surprised. "You're kidding."

"No." Though he might as well be, he thought. The idea of him inventing something that would revolutionize the industry now seemed a laugh. "I had a fuel cell that would have worked even better than the one in Vancouver. Had it just about ready to enter in a competition, but that explosion ended that plan."

"They have competitions for fuel cells?" She shook her head. "You men, you make everything into a competition."

"This is like a competitive bid. There's a car company in Detroit that will soon begin mass producing electric cars. It's going to make a decision the end of May on what type of fuel cell to use. I think the one I was working on would have been the most economical and would have produced more energy than anything out there. Now—"

He sighed, and she touched his arm. Tentatively. Almost as if she expected him to pull away, which he might have if the look on her face hadn't stopped him. She truly seemed to care. "You'll be back on your feet soon," she said. "Once those lacerations are healed, you'll be able to work on it again."

He shook his head. "From what the police said, everything in my lab is either in pieces or ashes. To have something ready by the deadline, I'd have to start working right away."

" 'Right away' might be a little too soon." She lifted

her hand from his arm. "Your uncle must have been afraid you might try that, though. He gave me explicit instructions not to let you go back to work too soon."

"He gave me the same instructions." Link remembered his uncle's admonition. *Don't push yourself*, he'd said. *Take a break. You always have next year.* "He worries about me. Fusses." Thinking about it, Link shrugged. "He's my only living relative. I've gotta be nice to him."

Annie laughed, the sound bubbly. "Must be rough on you."

The way she said it made him grin. "Terribly."

"Well—" She suddenly seemed unsure what to do or say next and stepped back. "Do you need anything more?"

"No." That she wanted to leave reignited his irritation. "Don't let me keep you from your book."

She glanced at the digital clock on his VCR. "Actually, I think I'd better get some sleep. I'll be checking on you in four hours, but if you need anything before then— a pain pill, water—anything at all, just call. Or push that buzzer your uncle rigged up. I'm a light sleeper."

"Don't worry about me. I'll survive."

"Yeah, the grumpy ones always do." She turned the light back down until there was only a soft glow, then she said a quick good night. He watched her until she was out of his sight, then he listened, following her footsteps down the stairs. His house had been invaded by a female. A feisty, back-talking woman. His life had been turned upside down.

He stared at the ceiling and wondered what Annie

Marsden would have said if he'd told her his dream. It had been about her. And he didn't need to talk about it to bring it into focus. Its meaning was clear. He'd dreamed she was leaving, leaving him helpless and alone.

And he'd bet she would—soon.

TWO

He twisted against the ropes binding his arms and legs. The chair creaked but didn't give. In front of him, on the table, sat the bomb. He could read the timer. Two minutes twenty-nine seconds. Twenty-eight. Twenty-seven. His life was ticking away.

—Time Bomb

Anne walked up the stairs smiling. She wouldn't say she'd had the best night's sleep—she never did sleep well in a strange bed, and she missed having her cat curled up beside her—but the sun was out and it was a beautiful day. As far as she was concerned, it was impossible not to smile.

"So you're still here," Link said when she entered the great room.

"I'm still here." She picked up a small flashlight and thermometer from the pile of equipment she'd left on one end table. "I know you're thrilled."

"I'll be thrilled when I'm out of this bed."

"A couple of weeks and you'll be bouncing around like a kid on a pogo stick."

"Sure I will."

The man was definitely a grouch, she decided. A good-looking grouch, but obviously determined to see his situation as bleak. Well, if he wanted the truth, she'd give it to him. "Okay, so maybe you'll be on crutches, but you'll be getting around. Once that side of yours heals, you'll be able to take care of yourself, and I'll be out of here."

"I can't wait."

She screwed up her nose and made a face, and for a moment she thought he was going to smile. But if he'd had the urge, it disappeared quickly. She directed the beam from the flashlight into his eyes, checking his pupil size. "So what's your name?"

"Oh, don't tell me we're going to do the 'What's your name, what day is it, and do you know where you are?' routine again."

"I just want to make sure those brain cells are working."

"Trust me, they're working. They're telling me you're a pain in the—"

He stopped at the lift of her eyebrows, and gave her the information she wanted. Convinced his neuro reactions were all right, she stuck the thermometer into his mouth and went to get the blood pressure cuff. He was watching her when she returned to the bed. He did have gorgeous eyes, she decided. Deep brown and velvety. Tempting eyes.

Except, she wouldn't be tempted. Their relationship couldn't be anything but professional. That went with the job. He was the patient; she was the nurse. No fraternizing.

She took his blood pressure and pulse, then pulled the thermometer from his mouth and read his temperature. "You pass," she said, and wrote the numbers on his chart.

"Oh, goodie. Do I get a gold star?"

She rewarded his sarcasm with a fake smile. "You get breakfast. Anything in particular you'd like?"

"A bloody Mary, steak and eggs."

"Well, you can't have the drink. No alcohol while you're on medication, and I'll have to check your freezer for the steak. But I do know you have some eggs in your refrigerator."

"Cereal's fine," he muttered.

"You're sure?"

"I wouldn't have said it if I wasn't sure."

Mornings were obviously not his best time. Nor evenings, if last night was any indication. With his "Don't fuss, don't pamper" rules, she wouldn't have any trouble thinking of him as a patient and not as an attractive man. "Any special cereal?"

"Whatever's out there."

She started for the kitchen, but paused to ask one more question. "Do you want coffee?"

"No," he said, then changed his mind. "Yes. But not that watery stuff I got in the hospital."

"In other words, make it strong. Black?" He nodded, and she wasn't surprised.

He drank his coffee like a "real" man. At least that's

what her father always said about men who preferred their coffee black and strong. She'd fix it that way, give Link what he wanted, then doctor hers with milk.

Annie continued on toward the kitchen, but stopped again just before she left the great room. "You said you were sure the explosion in your lab wasn't caused by what you were working on. Do you think it might have been caused by a bomb?"

"A bomb?" The question took Link by surprise. He tried to look at her—to see her expression—but the way the bed was positioned, he couldn't turn his head that far. He found it strange that she'd asked. He'd wondered the same thing himself, had even asked his uncle that question.

"You know," she went on. "Some kind of explosive device?"

"I know what a bomb is," he snapped. Darn, but she could irritate him. Even in the morning, she was all smiles and perky and bouncing around as if life was wonderful.

He didn't want to be jovial. "Why would anyone plant a bomb in my lab?"

"I don't know," she said. "I'm asking you. Do you have enemies?"

"Not that I'm aware of. I may not be the best-loved guy around, but I don't know of anyone who would want to kill me."

"Well, if your invention didn't blow up and a bomb didn't go off, what caused the explosion?"

"Don't you think I've asked myself that same question?" A million times, he was sure. "All I know is I walked into that room, started toward the fuel cell, and boom, all hell broke loose." Putting him in the hospital and now at her mercy. "And talking about it isn't getting me any coffee. Are you going to make some or what?"

"I'm going. I'm going."

He heard her huff with irritation, then moments later heard the sound of kitchen cupboards being opened and slammed shut. He knew from the way she was banging things around that his grumpiness had gotten to her.

So what are you trying to do, Sheffield? he asked himself. *Drive her off?*

Why not? he decided. She'd be gone soon enough anyway. Why not drive her off so he didn't get attached to those smiles of hers or the cute way she wrinkled her nose when she didn't like what he'd said. Maybe the next nurse the home care agency sent wouldn't be young and pretty, wouldn't put him on edge every time she came into the room.

After breakfast, Annie changed Link's dressing, helped him go to the bathroom, and gave him a sponge bath and his medication. It was midmorning before she renewed the conversation about the explosion. "Did you know that annually there are close to five thousand suspicious explosions in the U.S.?"

"Oh, really?" He turned his head on the pillow to look at her. She was poking around his stereo system, checking out his CDs.

She just didn't look like a nurse. Her uniform, if you could call it that, was a white lab coat over jeans and a red T-shirt. Her hair still looked as if it had been styled with an eggbeater, and her makeup was absolutely minimal. Not that she needed much makeup. With her, the natural look was enticing enough.

He decided he was definitely getting better. Every time Annie was around, he had a physical reaction to her. Considering how intimately she was getting to know his body, that was embarrassing.

"What is really amazing," she said, pulling out one more CD and putting it into his player, "is how many bombs are detected during airline passenger screenings. Around two hundred and fifty a year."

He watched her bend over to pick up a dropped CD case. The contour of her rear end was outlined by her lab coat, and he felt an explosive reaction within him. Quickly he looked up at the ceiling. "What are you, some statistics freak? Or is it just bombs that fascinate you?"

She straightened and turned toward him. "Actually, the reason I remember those numbers is because the mystery I was reading last night had a bomb in it, along with those statistics. It got me thinking. Five thousand explosions a year is a lot. But how many do you or I ever hear about?"

"The one I heard was enough."

"I suppose so." She pushed the button to start the music, then closed the CD cabinet. "You were the only one in the lab at the time of the explosion?"

"It was eleven-thirty at night. Yes, I was the only one there."

"Do you usually work that late?"

"Not usually, but that night I'd been at an awards dinner with my uncle. While the speeches were being made, I thought of something I wanted to check on in regard to the fuel cell. I was going to wait until morning, but on the way home, since I was only a few blocks away from the lab, I changed my mind and went there."

"Where is there?"

"Berkeley. Not far from the university campus."

"So you went to your lab at a time you aren't usually there, walked into the room, and bang?"

"That's about it." Maybe there was more, but he couldn't remember. He didn't remember anything from the time of the explosion until a paramedic was giving him oxygen. "Next thing I knew, I was being transported to the hospital."

The melodic strains of Leo Kottke's guitar filled the room, and Annie turned the music down so it merely provided a background, then she walked toward his bed. "What did the police say?"

"Not much, so far. They're supposed to have a report in a few days." Link found Annie's curiosity interesting. She was really into this, more even than the police detective who'd taken his statement. He'd had the feeling Detective Bronson had chalked the incident up to a mad scientist's experiment gone awry.

"Is there anyone else who would have had access to the lab?" Annie asked.

Detective Bronson had also asked that question. Link's answer was the same. "Diane Wilson. She's the grad student who's been working for me this year. But she was away. She won a cruise and left me to go have fun." It had annoyed him at the time. It still annoyed him.

Annie's eyebrows rose, and he had a feeling she had

picked up on his annoyance. "So, the night of the explosion, your lab assistant was on a cruise?"

"Yes, she'd just left that day."

"And do you give your assistant as bad a time as you've been giving me?"

He frowned. "What's that supposed to mean?"

"Do you boss her around? Grouch at her like you do me?" Annie hesitated for just a moment, then went on. "Would she have been upset enough with you to plant a bomb?"

He hadn't considered that possibility. Diane had been upset when he'd told her she might not have a job when she returned if she took that cruise. But what did she expect? He had a deadline, and she was taking off . . . just like a woman. On the other hand, was she upset with him to the point of planting a bomb? "No," he said, coming to his own conclusion. "She wouldn't do that. Heck, she's just a kid."

"How old a 'kid'?"

"I don't know. Twenty-two. Twenty-three." He lifted an eyebrow, looking at her. "You don't look much older than she does, especially dressed like that. I thought nurses wore white uniforms."

"Not always. I believe in dressing for comfort. Do you have a problem with what I'm wearing?"

The way he let his gaze travel down over the front of her T-shirt, Annie wished she hadn't asked that question. "No . . . no problem at all," he said, his gaze coming back to meet hers.

His tone revealed nothing of his thoughts, but the look in his eyes said volumes, most of it licentious. And the way that look made her stomach dance, she knew *she* had a problem. She didn't want to be attracted to him. He was too much like her ex, her father, and her brother. The studs. She wasn't interested in that type. At least, she shouldn't be.

"We were talking about Diane," she said, pulling her thoughts back on track. "She goes on a cruise and there's an explosion in your lab and everything you were working on was destroyed. Right?"

"Right. But if you're determined to turn this into some sort of mystery, you can forget Diane. What would she gain by blowing up my lab and destroying the fuel cell?"

Annie could name a dozen different possibilities she'd read in books. She gave him one. "What if she didn't really leave when you thought. She knows you're going to be at that awards dinner. She sneaks back after you've left the lab, takes your prototype and research papers, plants a bomb that's set to go off at eleven-thirty. She figures no one will realize she has your invention. She plans on selling the prototype and your papers to a foreign power, and doesn't know you went back to the lab."

"Sounds great except for two things."

"What?" The scenario had sounded good to her.

"First of all, we're not talking major nuclear weapon here. We're not even talking new power source. We're talking improvements."

"You said major improvements."

"Maybe, but . . ." He shook his head and smiled. "Second. When I walked into the lab, I saw the prototype and my papers. They were there, not with Diane. Besides,

I don't see her doing something like that. No foreign country would pay enough for that fuel cell to make it worth the risk to anyone."

"You're sure?" The fact that he'd seen the fuel cell did blow her theory, but an assistant could still have copies of his papers.

"Yes, I'm sure. I was working on a fuel cell for an electric car, not some—"

The phone rang, and Link stopped. The phone was within his reach, but he nodded at Annie. "You get it."

She grimaced at the curt order and picked up the phone. Immediately she smiled. If Link was the grumpy one, his uncle was Mr. Congeniality. "Ah, Mr. Sheffield," she said when he identified himself. "How are you?"

Link watched her face melt into a smile, and wondered what magic his uncle possessed. Women always melted around him, even the bristly ones. Not that it mattered, Link told himself. He didn't care if Annie fell under his uncle's spell. He didn't care about anything except getting better so he could get her out of his house and his life.

She twisted slightly so she was facing him. The smile stayed, along with a sparkle in her eyes. "Yes, he's fine," she said. "No, no problems. Sure."

She held the phone toward him, and Link took it. Why not? He was curious why his uncle was calling. The man was supposed to be on a plane to Minneapolis.

"It's your uncle," she said, stating the obvious.

"I thought you'd be gone by now," Link said into the mouthpiece.

❖━━━━━━━━━━❖

Ron Sheffield shifted position on the small seat of the airport pay phone booth. On either side of him were more of the open pay phones, all being used by men and women making last-minute calls before catching their flights. Over an intercom system the boarding procedure for a flight to Dallas was being announced. Ron knew he had twenty minutes until his plane began boarding. Even then, as a first-class passenger, he could go on at any time until they closed the doors.

His first stop would be Minneapolis/St. Paul. Two days of meetings there should have everything in order. His itinerary took him to Chicago next for more meetings. Boston followed Chicago, then London, Paris, and more cities than he could remember. All in all, he'd be away for nearly two months, but the trip should be profitable. Nevertheless, he had to make sure everything was okay before he left.

"Assuming the plane leaves on time," he said to Link, "I'll be out of here by eleven-thirty. You're feeling all right? You slept all right?"

As he listened to Link's answer, he fiddled with the chain on the telephone book. He smiled when Link began grumbling about having to have a woman around all the time, and reminded his nephew of how cute his nurse was. To be honest, Ron had been stunned when he opened the door and Annie Marsden had introduced herself as the home care nurse he'd ordered. He simply hadn't expected a nurse that young and good-looking.

"Play your cards right," he told Link, "and maybe you can get her to crawl into that bed with you."

He laughed at Link's response, and told him that abstinence was not likely to improve his temper. He was glad to hear the spirit in Link's voice, though. Two days earlier, he hadn't been sure Link would even live. Damn, that had scared him.

Why Link had gone back to the lab that night, Ron didn't know. As they were leaving the banquet, Link had said he was headed straight home. That's where Ron had gone. Straight home and to bed. He'd been sound asleep when the phone woke him at one in the morning. Nothing the police had said had made any sense at that hour. First of all, no one should have been at the lab. No one ever went to the lab at night.

He'd arrived at the hospital just as they were taking Link into surgery, and he'd been scared by his nephew's ashen pallor. It was after three before the doctor came out and assured him that Link would be all right, that they'd stopped the internal bleeding. The doctor added that Link would bounce back quickly. Ron wasn't surprised. Link was a lot like him. Resilient.

"Bomb?" he repeated, startled as Link's voice brought him back to the present. "Why do you think it might have been a bomb?" They'd discussed this once before.

As Link explained his reasoning, Ron looked toward the ceiling and blew out a frustrated breath. This wasn't good. Link shouldn't even be thinking about the explosion. He should simply relax and let his body heal.

"Look," he said, "forget this for now. What you need to do is concentrate on getting better. You've been push-

ing yourself as it is. That night of the awards banquet, you admitted that you were tired, that you hadn't been getting enough sleep. The condition you're in, you need to build up your resistance. Get your strength back."

"I can't just forget it," Link said. "Damn, I was so close."

"I know." Ron softened his tone. He could understand his nephew's frustration. "It's really a shame. But you're in no condition to work on that fuel cell. You lost a lot of blood. Had a concussion. Forget the fuel cell for this year. There's always next year."

"You make me sound half dead," Link muttered.

"You were half dead."

"You know, I still might be able to build another one before the deadline. In fact, with a little luck, I'm sure I could."

Stubborn, Ron thought. Link was as stubborn as his mother had been. Rachel couldn't be swayed. She might not have been around while Link was growing up, but genetically she'd given him her tenacity and pigheadedness. What worried Ron was that Rachel had also been unpredictable and had passed that trait on too. Before he left, he wanted to be sure that Link put all thoughts of the fuel cell aside and concentrated on taking care of himself.

"You listen to me," he said, adopting his most authoritative tone. "You are not to think about that fuel cell or the lab, not until you're back on your feet and one hundred percent all right. For the next month or two, you are to concentrate on getting better."

"You sound like my father," Link grumbled.

"Yes, I know. But with him gone, someone has to tell

you what to do. And I'm sorry I have to leave town right now." He chuckled. "Don't go and be too stubborn and run off that nurse. You may think you don't need her, but right now you do."

"Like hell I do."

"Yes, that's right, 'Like hell you do.' Look, I've got to go. I want to buy a paper before I get on the plane. I'll call as soon as I'm in Minneapolis and let you know what room I'm in at the Marriott."

Ron hung up the phone, picked up his briefcase, and started to walk away from the line of phones. He did want to get a paper. But before he'd taken two steps, he stopped and went back to the same phone he'd left. Using his credit card, he made another call.

"Detective Bronson?" he asked when the call was answered. "Ron Sheffield here. I'm calling from the San Francisco airport. My flight leaves in"—he checked his watch—"forty minutes. But before I leave, I wanted to talk to you about my nephew."

He waited for the detective's response before going on. "That's right. The one who was in the explosion in the lab. I'm worried about him." He dropped his voice, allowing his tone to take on a level of concern. "My nephew's condition isn't really all that good. I mean, with the loss of blood, concussion, and fractured leg . . . well, the doctors and I really feel what he needs is rest. I know you're waiting for a report on the cause of that explosion. I think maybe it would be better if you didn't give that to Link. At least, not right away. The less he has to think about right now, the better. Do you know what I mean?"

Ron smiled at the detective's answer. It was exactly what he'd wanted to hear. "Good. You give it to me, and when I think Link is strong enough, I'll tell him. I'll be at the Marriott in Minneapolis for the next two days. Then the downtown Hilton in Chicago after that. Once you have the report, you could call and leave a message, and I could get back to you."

He nodded, listening to the detective, then continued. "I'm glad you understand, and I agree with you. Probably just a case of his experiment blowing up."

"Your uncle is your only living relative?" Annie asked after Link had set the phone back on the table.

"Yeah." Link grunted. "He's worse than a maiden aunt. Always worrying about me. Don't do this. Don't do that."

"He cares about you." She came back to his side and straightened the covers. "Isn't it nice to know that someone does care?"

Link glared at her. "You're fussing again."

She raised her hands and laughed. "Sorry. Habit we nurses get into." She transferred her energy to picking up the newspaper he'd been looking at earlier. "I assume you did have parents at one time. What happened to them?"

"My mother left when I was four. Got tired of two kids, I guess. We never heard from her again. My father and brother were killed in a plane crash two years ago."

Annie stopped straightening the newspaper. "Oh, I'm sorry. That's terrible."

She expected him to grumble. Instead, he looked

away, toward the window that faced the bay. "Yes it was," he said softly, and she had a feeling the loss still gave him pain.

"Your uncle taking this trip—flying, I mean—that must make you a little nervous."

Link looked back at her, a slight frown crossing his brow. "Funny, I hadn't thought of that. Maybe because my father and brother were killed in a private plane. A Piper Cub."

"Those small planes scare me." Not that she'd ever flown in one.

"My dad always said they were safer than driving a car. He'd been flying for years and had never had a problem. I have no idea why his went down that day. He and Larry were just flying to a meeting in Monterey. The weather was good. There was no reason for the plane to crash."

"The investigators couldn't find anything?" It sounded like another mystery to Annie.

"The crash was caused by a mechanical error according to the FAA report, but I don't buy that. My father always checked out that plane. I can't imagine him missing anything, or going up if everything wasn't in tiptop condition, especially not with my brother in the plane. My dad was a risk taker, but he wouldn't do anything to jeopardize my brother's life. It just doesn't make sense to me."

"Sounds like two things have happened that don't make sense."

Link stared at her. "Two things?"

"The explosion in your lab and your father and brother's plane crash."

"I hadn't thought of it that way."

She saw a sadness in his brown eyes that touched her, stirring a desire to comfort him. It was there for just a moment, then it was gone. In its place came a frown. "You read too many mysteries. I'm tired. You go do whatever you nurses do. I'm going to take a nap."

She knew then that he wouldn't accept any comfort. "Real men" didn't need comfort. "Real men" didn't feel pain. Oh, boy, had she heard that enough times. They just *were* a "pain," she decided.

Annie shook her head and walked away. She would do what nurses did, she would care for him as a patient, but she wouldn't get emotionally involved with Link Sheffield.

THREE

The plane barely skimmed the mountaintop before going into a tailspin. Observers later told the authorities they saw the pilot eject. An extensive search was initiated, but the pilot wasn't found. Nor was the money he'd stolen from the Chase Manhattan Bank. That was why they called me onto the case. . . .

—The Heist from Heaven

Annie set the mystery magazine on the nightstand. The short story that had held her attention the night before had been different, the twist at the end unexpected. And maybe a three-page mystery with a plane crash in it had nothing to do with the plane crash that had killed Link's father and brother, but it had made her think about what he'd said. Actually, she'd been doing a lot of thinking about what Link had told her two days earlier.

Here she had relatives galore and did her best to escape them. Link had no one except his uncle. Though he said it didn't bother him, she was sure he was worried about his uncle flying. It would, at least in part, explain his grouchiness. Not that she was going to let her sympathies allow him to boss her around like a slave.

She'd lived with men like him—stubborn and bossy—had even foolishly married one. She'd learned the hard way that being a toad didn't gain a person respect . . . or fidelity.

More than once in the last two days, she'd gotten into an argument with Link. Mostly because she knew what she needed to get him to do and he didn't want to do it. She was sure he was cursing his luck for getting her as a live-in nurse. Well, she didn't think he was such a hot patient either. She would have preferred someone more appreciative and cooperative. Someone who didn't remind her that she had a weakness for his type of man.

Why she found Link attractive, she didn't know. Though his bruises were healing, his body taking on a less-battered look and proving her prediction that he was good-looking, she'd never considered physical appearance of primary importance. Personality. That's what she looked for in a man, and Link's personality ranged between grumpy and grumpier.

So why was it, when she'd helped him sit up on the edge of his bed the day before, and his arms slid around her neck in almost an embrace, she had felt her heart skip? And why did she latch on to the few times he did offer a thank you or anything that even resembled a compliment? Hadn't she learned anything from her marriage to Dennis?

As she finished straightening her bedroom, she considered the one Sheffield who was considerate and complimentary. Link's uncle called every day, checking on

Link's progress and letting him know where he was and what he was doing. He always took a moment or two to ask Annie how things were with her. She had a feeling he was afraid she might walk out on Link. Not that she would. The only "job" she'd ever walked out on was her marriage, and she wasn't really the one who'd strayed. If Link wanted her gone, he'd have to fire her.

The bedroom ready, she armed herself with a smile and headed for the stairs. It was time for another day of verbal battles.

By that afternoon, Link had threatened to fire her twice, and she had to admit, the idea of walking out on him was tempting. He'd been cranky all morning, snapping at her when she gave him a sponge bath, complaining when she made him get out of bed and sit in a chair while she changed his bedding, and yelling when she took the paper away before he was finished. Then at lunchtime, he'd complained about the soup she'd served. Now he was grouching about the physical therapy he had to do.

When the phone rang in the middle of his session, Annie considered ignoring it. She'd moved the phone earlier, over to the side table by the couch, so she could work closer to the bed. She knew she could now refuse to get it.

"Well, are you going to answer that or what?" Link asked.

"If I answer it and let you talk, will you stop fighting me over these exercises when you're done?"

He made a sound she chose to interpret as a yes, and she answered the phone. It was his uncle calling from Chicago. Going into the other room, Annie let Link talk in private, but as soon as she knew he'd hung up, she returned, ready to finish with his physical therapy.

Before she even reached the end of his bed, Link glared at her. "Look, can't we do this later? I'm tired."

She shook her head. "A promise is a promise, and even if you don't want to do the physical therapy for yourself, do it for your uncle."

"Let *him* do it for himself."

Annie suppressed a grin and slipped her hand under his cast at the knee joint. "Okay, like we've done before. Push down on your knee as if pushing against my hand."

He rolled his eyes, but she noticed a pressure against her hand and knew he was pushing. "Keep doing it," she urged, and hoped, if she distracted him with talk, they could get through his exercises in a reasonable manner. "You and your uncle are very close, aren't you?"

"Close enough." He continued pushing.

"He never married?"

"My uncle?" Link frowned, and she felt an easing up of pressure. "No. Why? You interested?"

She smiled at the idea. "If he were thirty years younger, maybe. He is a good-looking man. And most of all, *he* is considerate. Do it again. Press against my hand."

He grunted, but pressed. "Want to add rich?"

Link had missed her point about his uncle, and Annie shook her head. "Money has never been important to me."

"Oh, sure."

" 'Sure' is right," she said emphatically. "Don't tell me. Besides being a grouch, you're a cynic too? Now, flex your toes."

"I'm not a cynic." He flexed his toes. "I'm simply a man who knows the truth."

"The truth according to Dr. Link Sheffield. So now you have a doctorate in philosophy as well as physics?"

"A doctorate in the study of hard knocks."

"Ah, now we're getting down to the crux of the matter. So who dumped you?"

She had a feeling he almost answered, then he looked away. "We were discussing my uncle. Damn, now what are you doing?"

"Checking your circulation," she said, and stopped squeezing his big toe. Within two seconds, the color was back to normal. "Looks all right. Okay, who dumped your uncle?"

"I don't know. Some woman. Happened years ago, I guess. But if you think you have a chance with him, you'd better forget it. You may be cute, but I've seen prettier women try and fail."

She laughed. "I don't know if you realize it, but I think you just paid me a compliment. But just so you don't stay up nights worrying, I'm not going to fail because I'm not interested in trying. I was only curious."

Link had his own curiosity. He wanted to know why he'd felt an instant jealousy at the thought of Annie being interested in his uncle; and how he could be enjoying her touch even as she stretched muscles that didn't want to be stretched. That he was getting to like her—even her sharp tongue—bothered him. He didn't want to care.

"Neither my uncle nor I are the marrying type," he said, as much for his sake as for hers.

"Ah, what a shame." Judging from her grin, he knew she didn't care, and that illogically irked him.

She switched her attention to his left leg and made him bend his knee, then press his foot against her hand. He pushed and she resisted, and he could tell, from the way her lips were moving ever so slightly, that she was counting to herself. He found himself staring at her mouth, wondering how her lips would feel touching his, how she would respond to his kiss. Snapping his eyes shut, he tried to block out the thoughts. "Do we have to do this?"

"Yes, we have to do this." She eased his left leg down. "Rotate your foot to the left." He did, and she pushed against it, stretching the muscle more. "You're like a son to him, you know?"

"That's what he says." Link clenched his teeth against the burning ache in his unused muscles and decided there was no use fighting her. She was determined to torture him. Once again, he looked at her.

"Have you always been close to him?" she asked. She motioned for him to lift his left leg, and when he did, she slid her hand under his ankle, lifting the leg higher.

"Yeah." Link knew the routine. It was a lift, then down, then a lift again. He considered messing up her count, then decided, with his luck, he'd end up doing more instead of less.

"He said this trip was to keep the family business alive," she said, continuing the lifts. "That otherwise he wouldn't have left you in this condition."

Link wondered how a hip could get so stiff in just a few days. If suffering through these exercises had any positive benefits, it was that each lift tightened her T-shirt against her breasts. He could tell her nipples were hard. Problem was, his reaction to that bit of visual information was not beneficial. The sight of her rigid nubs hardened a part of his own anatomy, making lifting his leg all the more difficult.

"You all right?" she asked when he paused in a lift.

"Yeah," he lied, knowing nothing would be all right until he was on his feet and she was gone. She was just too tempting.

"What kind of business is your uncle in anyway?"

"The tool business," Link answered. "Sheffield's Tools. Every contractor, mechanic, and engineer's best friend. He and my father started the company back when they were in their twenties. Originally, Dad handled most of the day-to-day stuff while my uncle dealt with sales. When I got old enough, I helped a little, but my brother was the one who really got involved. He had a bunch of ideas he wanted to try, but then he and Dad were killed."

"Leaving your uncle as the sole owner?"

"Basically. I do own a share of the business. I'm what you would call a silent partner. Uncle Ron makes all the decisions."

He could almost see the wheels turning in Annie's head. She was going with what he'd said, mulling it over, and looking for a catch. Life, he was learning, was one big mystery story to her.

"And no," he said, interrupting her thoughts before

she got too carried away. "I don't think my uncle killed my brother and dad to take over the business."

"I didn't say he did." She looked surprised that he'd suggested such a thing.

"But you were thinking it."

"Well . . ." She hesitated. "Maybe just for a moment."

He'd known it. She was really quite transparent.

"Just for a moment," she insisted.

"If you say so." He'd accept that. "I just want you to realize that that plane crash and losing my dad and brother actually put the company in jeopardy, so it wouldn't have benefited my uncle. In fact, the company's precarious financial situation is why my uncle is on this trip. He's trying to shore up the accounts Sheffield's has and drum up some new ones. He's hoping that tapping into the foreign market will be the answer."

"I can see why he felt he had to go. I know—"

The doorbell rang. Annie looked in that direction, then back at him. "What is this? A conspiracy to keep you from doing your exercises? Were you expecting someone?"

"Not that I know of." But Link knew he would welcome a reprieve. His energy level was sapped and his muscles sore. "Get the door." She lifted an eyebrow, and he added, "Please?"

Annie smiled and eased his leg back down on the bed, then pulled the covers over him. "Very good. You remembered the magic word. There's hope for you after all."

Link doubted it. Much as he didn't want to, he liked this woman, smart mouth and all, way too much.

Standing on the landing was a slender man in his late twenties, his features Asian and his height average. The moment Annie opened the door, he smiled and held out his hand. "Hi, I'm Jeff Yamaguchi. I was one of Dr. Sheffield's students not so many years ago, and I also worked for him. Is he up to seeing visitors?"

Annie introduced herself and shook his hand. "He's not only up to seeing visitors, but he's probably going to bless you since you just got him out of his physical therapy."

"He's all right then?" Jeff looked concerned. "I heard his lab was completely destroyed."

"He's not in the best of shape, but he'll mend. Go on in." Annie pointed the direction to the great room and let Jeff go in by himself. She waited a few minutes, so they would have time to greet each other, before she entered the room.

Link had raised the bed and was in a seated position. Both men looked her way as she approached. "You've met the slave driver?" Link asked.

"Slave driver?" She scoffed at the idea. "You're the one who gives the orders. Get me this. Get me that."

"Do you think you could get us something to drink?"

"Sure." She looked at Jeff. "Coffee, tea, water, milk, or soda?"

"Iced tea would be very nice, thank you," he said politely.

"Same for me," Link said.

Annie went into the kitchen and poured the iced tea. She also found some cookies that she set on a plate. She could hear Link and Jeff talking. Jeff asked the usual questions regarding how Link felt and what had happened, then told Link how he'd heard about the accident and how saddened he'd been. They were on to Jeff's job by the time Annie brought in the tray with the iced teas and cookies. Jeff smiled as she approached, then looked at Link. "Your taste in women is improving."

Link snorted. "My uncle picked this one, and she may look sweet and adorable, but she's got a tongue as sharp as a knife."

"He brings out the worst in me," she said, handing Jeff a glass of iced tea. She gave the other to Link, then set the plate of cookies on the bed between them. "I really am sweet. My last patient even called me honey."

"He was probably asking for it," Link said, "hoping to sweeten you up."

Jeff laughed. "I guess nothing has changed. You're still picking on people." He looked at Annie. "He pretends he's a grouch, but he's really a marshmallow."

Annie doubted that and wasn't surprised when Link grumbled.

"When I first started working for him," Jeff went on, "he yelled at me all the time."

She knew the feeling. "And here I was taking it personally."

"I did not yell at you," Link said to Jeff. "And I don't appreciate being talked about as if I'm not here."

"You did yell at me," Jeff insisted. "I will never forget

that first day I came to work for you. I was scared to death. And in class, you had all of us so petrified, we were ready to drop by the end of the first class."

"I wanted to see if you could stand the pressure." Link looked at her. "He thought he was hot stuff then. I figured he needed a little humility."

Annie wondered how many other students and assistants Link had scared. Whereas he was sure he had no enemies, others might not share his opinion. She turned to Jeff. "Do you think he might have scared someone badly enough that they wanted to get back at him? Might have planted a bomb in his lab?"

"A bomb?" Jeff stared at her, then at Link. "Is that what happened? Someone planted a bomb in your lab?"

"That's her theory," Link said.

"And what is your theory?"

"I don't know. Maybe a gas leak in the building."

"Or maybe a disgruntled student," Annie repeated.

Jeff shook his head. "I don't think so. He scared a few, especially on the first day, and some would drop out, but those of us who stayed soon learned it was all a bluff. He's tough, but fair."

"And I haven't done any teaching for four years."

"But you have hired student workers," Jeff said.

"A woman named Diane who just happened to go on a cruise the same day the lab blew up," Annie told Jeff.

Jeff raised his eyebrows. "You hired a woman as an assistant?" he asked Link.

"A mistake, it seems. She's proven herself as undependable as any woman I've met. She wins a cruise and bang, she's gone. Doesn't matter that I'm in the middle of a project."

Jeff shook his head, smiling. "I don't believe it. You hired a woman."

"She was good," Link insisted, then looked at Annie. "And she didn't plant a bomb in my lab."

"How can you not consider it as a possibility?"

"Because the more likely possibility is a gas leak."

"Can't they tell?" Jeff asked. "Can't they make tests?"

"They are," Link said. "But it takes time for lab reports to come back."

"And when you get those reports, you'll see I'm right," Annie said firmly.

"Want to make a bet?" Link glared at her, and she glared back.

It was Jeff's laughter that pulled her attention to him. He was shaking his head. "Why don't you two save your arguing until you do get those lab reports?" He turned back to Link. "I heard you were working on a fuel cell. What happened to it?"

Annie left the room as the two discussed fuel cells. She kept herself busy in the kitchen, first cleaning up, then working on a cryptogram. She was there if Link needed her, but it bothered her that she'd gotten into an argument with him in front of his friend. She knew she shouldn't have. She was the nurse, not a friend or family member. When he had company over, she should be seen but not heard.

Up until it was time for Link's next dose of medicine, she stuck to that motto. Carrying pills and a glass of water, she walked back into the great room.

Jeff rose from his chair the moment he saw her. "I have stayed too long," he said apologetically to Link. "I've probably tired you."

"It's a good tired." Link glanced Annie's way. "Better than arguing with her."

"And I love you too," she said, forgetting her vow not to talk back in front of his friends.

"Don't give up," Jeff said as he stepped away from the bed. "If you decide you want to give it a try, I'll do anything I can to help. You know that. Just give me a call."

"It's a lost cause," Link said, shaking his head and pressing the control to lower his bed. "I might as well do as my uncle suggested. Forget it until next year."

Annie walked with Jeff to the door. He paused before leaving. "Keep arguing with him," he said. "He needs it. It worries me to see him like this. His giving up on that fuel cell isn't like him."

"His uncle feels it might be better for him to just wait until next year on that."

Jeff shook his head. "Next year may be too late. If you have something new and unique, you need to get it out there before someone else does. If he's come up with this design, someone else might too. There's always something better just waiting to be discovered. You take care of him. Okay?"

"Okay," she said, and watched Jeff get into the elevator that would take him up to ground level.

As she headed back into the great room, she considered Jeff's view of Link. It was certainly different from hers. He saw Link as a softy, as fair and compassionate. "Jeff thinks you're special," she said as she neared Link's bed. She automatically started to straighten the cover over Link's legs. At his glare, she pulled her hands back. "Sorry."

He looked away. "I'm not special."

"In his eyes, you're special. A regular marshmallow."

She wasn't surprised by the sidelong glance he gave her. It wasn't warm and friendly. "How are you feeling?"

"Tired."

He looked tired. "Why don't you try to take a nap. I probably should have scooted him out sooner, but you two seemed to be having a good discussion."

"The guy talks too much."

She didn't point out that Link had done his share of talking. Saying nothing, she headed for the stairway. She wouldn't mind a little time to herself. There was one more story in that mystery magazine she wanted to read. Then, in an hour, she would start dinner.

The moment Annie came back up the stairs, she noticed Link's bed was up. On his lap was the pad of paper and a pencil that had been lying on the table near him. He was busy writing, and she wasn't even sure he heard her come into the room. "I take it you're rested," she said, easing close enough to see what he was writing.

He looked at her, a brightness in his eyes she hadn't seen before. "I got to thinking," he said, and even his voice was more energized. "Jeff's right. So the fuel cell was destroyed, along with my notes. It's not like my brain was destroyed. I've got it here." He tapped his head. "What I created once, I can create again. And since I've done it once, I won't make the same mistakes. It won't take me as long this time. There's no reason why I can't have another one ready in time for the competition deadline."

Annie stared at him, amazed by the change. In his eyes, she saw the dream. In his voice was the hope. He had a challenge, and he was going to meet it.

Oh, how he reminded her of her father and brother. Just give them a challenge and they were ready. It was that competitive spirit. They had to be the best, had to be the winners. Link would create a better mousetrap, or in this case a better fuel cell. Mr. Fix-It was alive and well, and from the looks of him, about ready to jump off his bed and go to work, whether his body was ready or not.

"Whoa," she said, putting up her hands. "I think this was what your uncle was trying to warn me about. You need to take this slow and easy. Your side is getting better, but your body still needs time to heal."

He grinned and caught hold of her hand. "Now, aren't you the one who wanted me exercising, who told me we had to keep the muscles stretched and limber? I'm exercising my mind."

He was also exercising *her* mind. She didn't understand how the simple touch of his fingers could get her pulse racing, but hers was going wild. She looked down at his hand, his long fingers completely encircling her small wrist.

He also looked in that direction, but he didn't release his hold. Instead, he moved a finger, stroking her skin. "I can feel your pulse."

That wasn't what she wanted to hear. "Oh, yeah?"

She swallowed hard, refusing to acknowledge that his touch was affecting her.

His smile widened. "Yeah."

Annie licked her lips, unsure what to say. He was looking at her, his gaze intense and boring straight into her soul. She wanted to look away, to pull her arm free. Instead, she didn't move.

He let her go, releasing his hold as quickly as he'd taken it and returning his hand to the paper on his lap. "Think you could find me a hard surface to write on?" he asked. "Maybe a tray or something? Please?"

It was the please that got to her, and his smile. She backed away from his bed. "I'll find something," she said, and nearly tripped over her own feet. "Then . . . then I think I'll start dinner."

He watched her, his head cocked slightly, just the hint of a smile remaining on his lips. Annie hurried to the kitchen, found him a tray and brought it to him, then rushed back to the kitchen. There she leaned against the counter and took in several deep breaths, all the while chastising herself. She would not let herself consider what had just happened. So her pulse started racing when he touched her. Big deal. It meant nothing. It couldn't mean anything. She had to have learned something from her marriage to Dennis. Getting the hots for a man who wanted to be the best only led to heartache. There was always a challenge, mountains to climb, women to conquer.

She had to have learned something.

FOUR

The Inspector stared at the body lying on the bed. The victim, according to the coroner, had been dead for several hours, placing the time of the murder close to midnight. They had a name, at least the one the victim had registered under, and they had a weapon, though the Inspector doubted they'd find any prints on the knife. What they didn't have was a means. From what he'd been told, there was no way anyone could have gotten into or out of the room at the time of the murder. The windows were locked and the door had been locked and chained shut from the inside.

—The Briefcase Murders

Annie always loved "impossible entry" mysteries. Like the cryptograms she played with in her spare time, the challenge of finding the solution was fun. She leaned back against the pillow on her bed and began to read the magazine's short story.

The ring of the telephone startled her, and she

glanced at the clock. It was after ten, but she knew Link was still awake. She'd left him only a short while ago, busy working on his notes. Ever since Jeff Yamaguchi's visit that afternoon, Link had been preoccupied with the fuel cell—making sketches and jotting down ideas.

She also knew he could reach the telephone, since she'd left it on the table near his bed. She wasn't surprised when the second ring was abruptly cut off. Nevertheless, she slipped off the daybed and stepped out of her room. For a moment she stood at the base of the curving stairs, listening. If there was a problem, she wanted to be aware of it. Although Link was healing nicely and gaining strength daily, he didn't need any bad news or shocks. Long ago she'd learned a patient's mental attitude played as important a role in recovery as any medicine the doctors might prescribe.

"No, it's not too late, Uncle Ron," she heard Link say. "Just working on some notes. She's downstairs. No, everything is fine."

Satisfied that it was simply his uncle's daily phone call, Annie went back to her room and the mystery she was reading.

Upstairs, as his uncle talked, Link continued sketching. For most of the evening, he'd been reconstructing the specs he'd used for the fuel cell, but after Annie went downstairs, he'd started sketching something else. On the paper in front of him was the curvy figure of a woman.

Link didn't consider himself particularly good at drawing people. They usually ended up looking like cartoon figures, but he was pleased with the way this one was taking form. Not that anyone else would ever see it.

When he was finished, he'd destroy the drawing. He definitely didn't want Annie finding it.

Maybe she wouldn't recognize the woman in the drawing as herself. Then again, in his opinion, the long, slender legs, small rear end, and flat stomach should be a dead giveaway. He continued drawing, sketching in voluptuous breasts. For a moment he gazed at them, then grinned and erased them and made them smaller. He was a realist.

The neck he drew was long and graceful, and for her face, he used an oval. The nose was an upward tilting stroke, dots created the eyes, and arched curves over those dots became the eyebrows. He brought her hair to life by pressing the edge of the pencil onto the paper and making short, sassy strokes. He'd left the mouth until last and was about to start on that when he realized his uncle had said something and was waiting for a response.

"Yes, yes, I'm listening." Link glanced at the drawing and tried a short, curved line for the mouth. "You were saying you think you've convinced TriCon to go with Sheffield's. That's good. Glad to hear it."

His uncle responded, and Link tried making the line for the mouth a little thicker. He wasn't getting it right, and that bothered him. He wasn't capturing the way she could look at him with that slight upturn of her lips and make his thoughts turn crazy.

"What?" Link realized he'd missed something else his uncle had said. "No, no. I'm listening, really I am."

He grinned at his uncle's answer to that. The man knew him too well. But he'd bet his uncle didn't know what was sidetracking him from the conversation, and

Link certainly wasn't going to tell him. "Yes, I guess my mind is on something else," he admitted, grinning at the picture. Then he looked over at the other drawings he'd been making during the evening. "I'm working on my fuel cell plans."

"You're what?" Ron Sheffield sat down on the edge of his hotel bed.

He knew he had his nephew's full attention now, but he didn't like what he was hearing. "I thought you'd agreed to forget the fuel cell, at least for now. It hasn't even been a week since that explosion. You've been through major surgery. Had a concussion. Have a fractured leg. You need to be resting."

He looked at his watch and calculated the time difference between Chicago and California. "I shouldn't have called you this late. You should be asleep. What's wrong with that nurse of yours anyway?"

Ron remembered back to the woman he'd left in charge of Link. He'd been concerned when he first saw her. She looked so young. Certainly not what he'd expected in a home care nurse. He'd been prepared to open the door to a nurse in her fifties or sixties. Someone who'd done her time at a hospital. A widow or divorcee whose kids were grown and who was looking for part-time work. Someone with maturity and experience.

Instead, the agency had sent a charmer, a woman barely out of her teens who was all smiles and energy. He hadn't complained. There hadn't been time to get anyone else. And, to be honest, he'd thought Miss Cute-as-can-be might be good for Link, might keep his mind off what had happened.

Link's next comment jolted Ron up off the bed. "What do you mean, she thinks what you're doing is fine?" Carrying the phone with him, Ron walked over to the dresser. He'd already loosened his tie and unbuttoned the top buttons of his shirt. Now he jerked the tie off, all the while listening as Link described a visit from a former student and assistant.

"Just forget that damned fuel cell," Ron demanded, interrupting Link. "You were in an explosion. You were nearly killed." And that had scared the hell out of him. "You need time to recover. You can build that fuel cell next year. There's—"

"Don't put off until tomorrow what you can do today," Link said, and Ron grimaced. The adages he'd quoted to Link while the boy was growing up were coming back to haunt him.

"Besides," Link added, "Annie thinks it's good for me."

"Good for you?" Ron repeated. "She said that?"

There was no question about it. He had to get that woman away from Link. She was goading him on, undermining everything he was trying to accomplish. "I don't care what she said," Ron stated, slowly and deliberately. "You heard what the doctor said before he released you from the hospital. You are to take it easy, get lots of rest, and let that body heal. Now put those fuel cell plans away and go to sleep. I'll call you tomorrow."

He hung up the phone and stared into the mirror. He had to do something. He couldn't leave things as they were. Next thing he knew, this nurse would have Link thinking he could have that fuel cell ready to enter in the competition for the EV5 model.

What Link needed was a nurse who wouldn't kowtow to him, someone who would see to it that he stayed in bed and got his rest, who wouldn't feed his wild ideas. He needed that older woman, someone Ron could talk to and convince that Link needed to rest.

He went to his briefcase and flipped through his appointment book. Five days back, he found the listing and phone number he'd been looking for. He knew the Glencove Home Care Agency wouldn't be open, but he also knew they had an answering service. Tonight he would leave a message—get the ball rolling—and in the morning, when he called back, he'd get some action.

The phone rang at ten o'clock the next morning, and Annie hurried to pick it up in the kitchen. Link had said he didn't want to be disturbed. He was back working on his notes, making calculations, then scratching them out and starting over. He'd asked her to screen all calls.

When she answered the phone, she discovered the call was for her, not him. Lois Greenman, the director of Glencove Home Care, was on the other end of the line. Her greeting was stiff and formal, and Annie immediately sensed something was wrong. As she listened, her emotions switched from surprise to shock to anger. By the time she hung up, she was furious. Ready for battle, she headed for the great room.

"Thanks," she said bitterly, stopping beside Link's bed.

Seated on the bed with his tray of papers lying across his thighs, he looked up from his mathematical figures. Most of his bandages had been removed, his cuts and bruises now in various stages of healing. The one on his forehead still had a purplish tinge, and a lock of his unruly hair had fallen across the area. He pushed the hair back, then flinched when he touched the tender skin, but said nothing.

"You men," she ground out, too furious to care what she said. "You think you're God's gift to women, that we should jump the moment you open your mouth, bow before you and thank you for the tidbits that you throw us. Just because you're good-looking and smart, you think everything should revolve around you. Don't touch. Don't fuss. Get me this. Do that—"

He looked confused, but she didn't let that stop her. "Yes, I talk back to you, but don't tell me you don't deserve it. You and all your grumbling and grouching. Maybe you are some big inventor with lots of money, but that doesn't give you the right to be a pain in the ass. Ever since I got here, you've whined about your situation and snapped at me, as if I caused it. Well, let me tell you, bad things happen. So your mother walked out on you when you were a kid. And your father and brother were killed in a plane accident. I'm sorry for you. Really I am. But that doesn't give you the right to act like an overbearing boor. If you were any sort of a man, you would have told me to my face that you wanted me out of here. But no, you have to call my boss, tell her I'm incompetent. Tell her—"

"Whoa!" Link held up his hand, frowning as he tried to put together everything she'd said.

"No, I won't 'whoa,'" she snapped back. "If you don't like hearing the truth, well too bad. I am not incompetent. I went through nursing school at the top of my class. Maybe I don't have a Ph.D., but I'm not dumb. I know my job, and I've done my job here, in spite of all the times you've ordered me to go away or stop. If you think getting someone else in here will solve all of your problems, then I really feel sorry for you. Oh, sure, you may find someone who will grant all of your wishes and not talk back. I'm sure that's what you asked Mrs. Greenman to find in my replacement, but—"

"What replacement?" he asked, still totally in the dark.

"The one who is coming this afternoon to take my place," Annie said. "The one you requested this morning. Requested because I was incompetent."

She spit out the last few words, and Link saw the fire and anger in her eyes. For a moment, he wondered if the explosion in his lab had affected his mental capacities, because he was having trouble understanding what she was saying. "What call?"

"The one you made to the home care agency this morning."

She stood beside his bed, battle ready, her shoulders squared and her jaw rigid. Even her nostrils were flared, and he could practically feel the darts she was throwing from her eyes. He admired her willingness to fight for what she believed in, but he knew she was wrong in attacking him. "I didn't make any call to the home care agency. Not this morning or at any time. I don't even know the number."

"Oh, yes you do." She pointed at a note his uncle had left him. It was on the table beside his bed.

He remembered then that Ron had said the home care agency's name and number were on the paper, along with his uncle's travel itinerary. He picked up the paper and saw the phone number, then set the paper back on the table. "Okay, it's here, but I didn't make any call there."

"If that's your story, fine. But someone did, and the result is I'm canned. My replacement will be here this afternoon. I'm sure they'll find someone you can boss around."

She started to turn away, and Link grabbed for her arm, leaning forward and twisting as he did. He caught her by the wrist, but the movement pulled the muscles along his side and a sharp pain stabbed through his body. He gasped, but he didn't loosen his hold. Lying back against the pillow, he drew Annie close to the bed. "I do not want someone I can boss around," he said, gritting his teeth and waiting for the pain in his side to subside. "I did not call the home care agency. Not this morning. Not last night. Not at any time. I have no idea what you are ranting and raving about."

"I am not ranting and raving."

"Could have fooled me." He watched her absorb what he'd said. Slowly the anger left her eyes, her jaw relaxing slightly. When he thought she would listen, he went on. "Now, start at the beginning. I gather this is because of that phone call you just got. What was said?"

She didn't answer right away, simply looked at him. He could feel her pulse through his fingertips. Her heart was pounding, but he knew this time it wasn't from his touch but from the adrenaline pumping through her arteries. He could also see the rapid rise and fall of her chest. That finally began to slow, and she settled down enough to give him the information he needed. Even her tone was softer when she spoke.

"That call was from Lois Greenman, the director of the Glencove Home Care Agency. She's my boss. She said you'd called last night and left a message that you wanted to talk to her. Then you called again this morning, a little over an hour ago. You said you were dissatisfied with my services, that I was incompetent, and you wanted me replaced, immediately. She said she'd spent the last hour contacting people and had finally found someone, and my replacement would be here this afternoon."

Link watched Annie as she told him what had happened. Considering what she was saying, he could understand her anger. If he'd been in her position, he would have been furious. When she finished, she looked at him, challenging him to deny what he'd done. That wasn't difficult. "I didn't make either of those calls, Annie."

"Oh, yeah? If not you, who?"

He intended to find out. "You stay here." He lifted her arm slightly, then released his hold on her wrist, watching her as he did. To his relief, she didn't move, simply let her arm fall back to her side.

Reaching over to the table, he picked up the phone and the paper his uncle had left. Quickly he punched in the numbers for the home care agency, then waited for the connection. Leaning back against the pillows, he glanced at Annie. She was watching him, nervously licking her lips. He wondered if she had any idea how cute she looked when she was angry. All spit and fire. He wondered if she had any idea how cute she looked all the time.

A staff member answered the phone and he asked for the director. Within seconds he was connected to Lois Greenman and identified himself. Her response was hesitant, and he went directly to the point. "What the hell is going on?"

She repeated, almost verbatim, what Annie had told him. That she'd found someone to replace Annie and that person would be at his place that afternoon. She added that she was very sorry that Annie hadn't worked out, that they had had a couple of complaints about Annie talking back to patients, mostly from relatives, not from patients themselves, but that she was very competent and they had thought she would work out.

He put an end to that misconception. "She's working out very well, thank you, and I do not want her replaced."

Lois Greenman began backtracking, clearing her throat as she did and making excuses. It took a while, but Link got the gist of what she was saying and it didn't make him happy. "My uncle may have made the initial arrangements for a live-in nurse for me, but that was because at the time I was in no condition to do so myself. I am now quite capable of handling my own affairs, and I will be handling this situation. Your bill will be paid by me, and if you replace Ms. Marsden, I will not be paying.

If you have any doubts about that, check your records. I'm sure it is my insurance and my name listed as the one responsible for payments, not my uncle."

From the rustle of papers that he heard in the background, Link was sure she was doing just that. He waited, giving her time to confirm what he'd said. Meanwhile he kept watching Annie. Her back was no longer rigid, her posture more at ease. He could tell she was listening, waiting. Reaching out, he touched her arm, running a fingertip over her skin. Her eyes widened, but she didn't move her arm, and he smiled. Lois Greenman responded then, and he drew his hand away from Annie.

"Yes," he said, answering the director. "Oh, I can understand." The woman wanted some kind of confirmation that he was who he said he was. He gave her information he knew she would be able to check against his paperwork. Information that others would not be likely to know, such as his mother's maiden name, and that he'd been allergic to milk as a child. After that, the director's attitude changed. Money, he'd learned, did have power.

Link didn't waste any time stating his position. "I am perfectly happy with Ms. Marsden. She is exactly what you said, efficient and competent. I don't know where my uncle got the impression that she wasn't doing her job. I think she's doing a wonderful job."

He chuckled as the director repeated what his uncle had said that Link had said about Annie. Maybe he shouldn't blame his uncle for this, he mused. Ron might have thought he was doing what was right. Link tried to explain. "I may have said that to my uncle, but I have a tendency to grumble about all women, and I can't say I've been particularly happy with the situation I've found my-self in, but that can't be blamed on Ms. Marsden, now, can it?"

As she listened to Link defend her to her boss, Annie struggled to make sense of everything that was going on. One moment she'd thought she'd been fired. Now it looked as if she still had her job. She'd been angry as all get out with Link, but what she was hearing from him now were compliments. And the way he'd touched her, stroking his finger down her forearm . . . That touch, so light and intimate, had set off an onslaught of electrical sparks. And the way he'd looked at her with those deep brown eyes of his. That smile of his. She didn't know what to make of it. Inside, she felt all giddy and excited. In her head, though, she was confused.

"Good," Link said into the phone. "Then it's under-stood? Ms. Marsden stays. You'll call and cancel that re-placement? And if there are any problems, I will be the one who makes the complaints." He paused, and Annie knew he was listening to her boss's response. Then he spoke again. "No, no problems. I understand the misun-derstanding. My uncle thought he was doing what was right. He simply didn't understand. Thank you."

Once he'd hung up the phone, he looked at Annie. "Now, as for you . . ."

Every cutting word she'd said to him flashed through her mind. She grimaced, remembering. "I suppose I should thank you."

"I suppose you should." He watched her closely, his expression somber. "A pain in the ass?"

She bit her lower lip, wishing she'd kept her mouth

shut earlier. Problem was, she'd meant everything she said. "Sometimes you are."

He chuckled. "God's gift to women, huh? Good-looking?"

"As if you didn't know," she said, certain that women were always falling at his feet.

"I think there was an overbearing boor in there too."

She grimaced, afraid that might have been a little strong.

"I'm surprised you didn't add obnoxious."

"No." She shook her head firmly on that. "I wouldn't call you obnoxious."

He said nothing, but the way he was looking at her, those dark eyes of his penetrating so deep into hers, unnerved her. Could he tell how much he fascinated her? she wondered. Did he have any idea how difficult it was for her to maintain a professional attitude around him?

He was anything but obnoxious, and that was the problem. Unable to maintain the eye contact, she looked away.

"So is everything all right now?" he asked, the mockery gone from his tone. "You're satisfied I didn't make that call?"

"I'm satisfied." She looked back, one question still unanswered. "But why does your uncle want to get rid of me? I thought he liked me."

Link shrugged. "I don't know. All I can guess is I've called you sassy and said that you boss me around and talk back. Maybe he thought you were out of line."

"I suppose I do get out of line at times." She knew she

should watch what she said more and definitely had to watch how she reacted around him.

"No doubt about it," Link said, his gaze on her face and his smile soft and warm. Then quickly he looked away. "And don't go thinking, just because I made that call, that I think you're the greatest nurse around or that I'm wild about having you here. I just didn't want to have to go through the process of training someone new. Now, go busy yourself somewhere else. You've wasted enough of my time this morning. I've got work to do."

Annie chuckled to herself as she walked back to the kitchen. Things were back to normal. Then she remembered his touch and look, and knew she was wrong. Something had happened that morning, something she couldn't explain. Normal had taken a new direction.

FIVE

As she pedaled her bike through Cabot Cove, the mystery writer thought about the lab reports she'd just seen. She now knew, without a doubt, who the killer was, and she needed to warn—

—Murder, She Wrote

Ron Sheffield snapped off the television. He'd wanted news, not the rerun of a mystery show. Grabbing his briefcase, he headed for the door. He had ten minutes until his luncheon appointment with Archer Weirs, President and CEO of Weirs Manufacturing. Plenty of time to get down to the lobby.

Before he reached the door, the telephone on the stand by the bed rang. For a moment he hesitated, then turned toward the phone. He hoped that wasn't Weirs canceling. He needed to see that man.

To his surprise, the voice on the other end of the line

was Link's, and from Link's tone, Ron knew why his nephew was calling. Link's first words confirmed it.

"Yes, I made that call," Ron answered, not bothering to deny it. "And no, I don't think I was out of line."

He'd hoped there wouldn't be a problem. After all, Link had been grumbling about Annie Marsden from the moment he'd laid eyes on her. "You said she irritated you," he reminded Link. "That she talked back and didn't take orders."

"Just because I get upset with her doesn't mean she's not doing her job," Link said. "Problem with her is she does her job too damn well."

"Okay, so she's not incompetent. I still think you need someone else there."

"Why?"

"Why? I'll tell you why. The doctor told you to take it easy. I told you to take it easy. But last night when I called, what do I hear? She's encouraging you to work on the fuel cell."

"Because she knows I'm going out of my mind just lying around here. Uncle Ron, you're being a little ridiculous about all of this."

"No, I am not being ridiculous. Look, you've brought it up in the past, and I've been thinking about it. That explosion could have been caused by a bomb. And if someone planted a bomb in the lab, it means you're working on something they don't want you working on. And what have you been working on for the last six months?"

There was a moment of silence, then Link answered, "The fuel cell."

"Right. And if you go back to working on that fuel cell, you could be putting your life in danger. Think about it, Link. In your condition, if there was another attempt on your life, what could you do?"

Link heard the concern in his uncle's voice, and although the idea of someone trying to kill him because of a fuel cell was absurd, he could see how Ron might jump to that conclusion. He tried reassuring him. "Uncle Ron, think about it. Why would anyone want to stop me from developing a fuel cell? Certainly not the major car manufacturers. They might try to buy me out, but they wouldn't resort to bombs."

As Link had expected, his uncle agreed that he was right. Perhaps reluctantly, but he still accepted the logic of Link's reasoning. Nevertheless, Ron continued expressing concern that Annie was goading him into doing more than he should in his present condition. His uncle didn't realize how wrong he was, and Link assured Ron that Annie watched over him like a hawk. She was not going to let him overdo.

His uncle muttered another warning, and Link chuckled. "Yes, I know this rest is good for me. Look, if it makes you feel any better, I'll take it easy until I go to the doctor's in five days. I think it's a morning appointment. Annie has all that information in the file the doctor left for her."

As Link expected, his uncle sounded relieved. He even made a joke about Link lowering his standards to ride in Annie's Geo. Link hadn't pictured Annie driving a Geo, and when his uncle said it was a Geo Metro, Link knew he wasn't riding in it. Annie's car would be about as big as a golf cart. No, he told his uncle, they'd be going in the Jaguar.

He laughed when his uncle called him a snob and stubborn. "I am also overbearing and obstinate and God's gift to mankind." He remembered Annie had called him good-looking as well. For some reason, that pleased him. Considering his physical condition and the cuts and bruises on his face, he didn't see how she could say that. But she'd been angry at the time, and he didn't think she'd have blurted it out if she hadn't meant it. She found him good-looking, and he liked that. Liked it a lot.

"Speaking of tired," he said, smiling to himself, "I need to get some rest before the bully comes in. She's talking about getting me up on crutches today. Just 'for a bit,' she said, but her bits last longer than mine. You take care, okay?"

After he'd hung up, Link lowered his bed until it was flat. He was tired, but it was a good tired. He'd made progress on re-creating the designs for the fuel cell, and he'd settled the problem with Annie.

Then again, maybe he'd only initiated a problem with Annie. Their relationship had changed that morning. He'd admitted that he liked having her around, and she'd admitted that she thought he was good-looking. And he knew from the way she reacted whenever he touched her that some kind of chemistry was working between them. If he were truly smart, he would have let the home care agency replace her. Keeping Annie around could be dangerous. Her presence was explosive.

Annie answered the doorbell when it rang that afternoon. For a moment she feared Link hadn't canceled the replacement and she was going to find another live-in nurse standing on the stoop, there to take her place. When she swung open the door, however, it was a man she saw. A man six feet plus in height, lanky and middle-aged, wearing jeans and a T-shirt, and smiling. He immediately held out his hand. "Hi, I'm Dan Zura, and you must be Annie. Link told me you'd be answering the door." Dan looked beyond her, into the house. "He called me a while ago. Said he wanted to see me. Where you keeping the bum?"

"He's in the great room," Annie said, not quite sure what to make of the situation.

"Good." Dan eased past her. "I know my way."

He headed for the great room, his long legs covering the distance in an ambling gait, and Annie closed the door behind him and followed, taking her time. She paused at the doorway and listened as Dan and Link greeted each other, Dan standing back to look at Link, then making a few comments about how ugly Link looked. She could tell the two men had been friends for a long time. Only when Dan had pulled a chair up beside Link's bed did she enter the room. As soon as Link saw her, he formally introduced Dan. "Dan and I have worked together on several projects," he added. "Sharpest guy I know. Think you could get us something to drink?" He turned to Dan. "You still downing those diet things?"

Dan looked at her. "Do you have any diet cola?"

"There are some in the refrigerator." She glanced Link's way. "And for you, O master?"

"I'll take my caffeine in a coffee." He nodded slightly. "Please."

She nodded back and went into the kitchen to get the drinks. When she returned, Link was showing Dan his sketches. Dan looked up as she approached, smiled, and took the glass of cola she offered. "Here's the one who's smart," he said, gesturing toward Link. "I hope you do know you're taking care of a certified genius. I don't even begin to come close to him."

"Now, don't go pumping up my ego," Link said, looking at her, not Dan. "She thinks I'm obnoxious enough as it is."

"I never said you were obnoxious," she corrected him, and knew her best bet was to stay out of the conversation. "If you'll excuse me, I have work to do."

She heard them laughing when she left the room, but she didn't linger. Going downstairs, she tossed Link's bedding into the washer and started the machine. Being a live-in involved far more than nursing. She was cook, maid, and general gofer. Once the washing was going, she took two letters Link had written earlier that day up to the mailbox.

Dan Zura stayed for an hour, then Annie interrupted them, suggesting an end to the visit so Link could get some rest. Link grumbled at the idea, but only halfheartedly. He hated to admit how easily he did tire. He listened as Annie let Dan out, then closed his eyes when she came back into the room. He could sense when she was close to the bed. There was the scent of her perfume, light and subtle, along with a personal aroma that mingled with the soap and shampoo she used. He could also feel her presence in the air, an energy that triggered a tension within him. Anticipation vibrated from nerve ending to nerve ending, a hope that she would touch him mingling with a fear that she might. He pretended he was asleep and felt her straighten the blanket over him. She fussed, and he didn't really mind. But he knew her presence in his life was only temporary. Another week and she'd be gone. It seemed like anyone he ever cared about left. It was safer not to care.

She continued standing beside him, and he wondered what she was doing, but he didn't open his eyes, didn't let her know that he was aware of her presence. Keeping his breathing slow and even, he pretended he was asleep. Finally she left . . . and he let out a sigh of disappointment.

It was evening when they had a chance to talk. Annie had given him his medicine, taken his temperature and blood pressure, and written everything in his chart. She had him sitting in the easy chair she'd pulled over next to his bed. She'd said he needed to be out of bed for a while. She'd gotten him up on crutches for a few minutes, but the pull on his side had been too much and they'd agreed to wait another day or so before trying again.

So he sat in his chair and watched her busy herself straightening this and that. She glanced at the drawings lying on his table, then looked at him. "Are you really a certified genius?"

Considering that he was allowing himself to get emotionally attached to another woman, Link figured certifiable idiot was probably a better description, but he nodded. "That's what I'm told."

"So what's your world like? I mean, being a genius, do you see things differently from others?"

"I don't know." Her frankness fascinated him. "I don't know how you see things, so how can I make any comparison?"

"I guess you're right." She walked around his hospital bed, then sat down on the carpeting in front of him, crossing her legs. "I suppose you got A's all through school, took all those accelerated classes."

He nodded, then smiled, remembering back. "I did get a B in gym class once."

"Aw, poor boy. Did you play any sports in high school?"

"Couldn't. I started college when I was fourteen."

Her eyebrows shot up. "You're kidding."

He wasn't. "Had my doctorate degree when I was twenty-two."

She laughed, dimples forming in her cheeks. He liked it when she laughed, liked it when she shook her head, her hair moving softly from side to side. He had an urge to lean forward and touch her hair, to feel its softness. He quelled that urge.

"Your world is most definitely different from mine," she said, still grinning up at him. "At age twenty-two, I was just starting college and in the final stages of a divorce. A divorce decree is not exactly the same as a Ph.D."

"No, I guess not." Her comment about her divorce made him curious. "What happened? Marriage not quite what you expected?"

"I guess you could say that. I had this delusion that marriage was a partnership based on mutual respect and trust." She scoffed. "Dennis figured those wedding vows meant I cooked his meals, cleaned his house, and looked the other way while he had one affair after another."

Link grimaced. It didn't take a genius to get the picture. "Your husband was unfaithful."

"He was a jerk." She blew out a breath, and Link saw the same fire in her eyes that he'd seen that morning when she'd come storming into the room, accusing him of being a jerk. "I gave him two chances," she said. "I think that was more than enough. When he started sleeping with my best friend, I left. No more working for minimum wage so he could spend my money on other women."

"That's when you decided to become a nurse?"

She nodded. "Actually, I wanted to be a doctor, but I come from a family where a woman's intelligence isn't held in high esteem. Even deciding to be a nurse was a big step for me. It took a good friend to convince me that I had a brain."

"So why do you do this home care nursing? Why aren't you working in a hospital or doctor's office?"

"When I first graduated, there were no openings in any of the hospitals, at least not in any of the areas I wanted. Still, the bills needed to be paid, so I signed up with Glencove. And lo and behold, I discovered I liked this kind of work. Maybe it's knowing I can turn down a job if I want, though I haven't so far. And they've kept me busy. I haven't even had time for a vacation." She cocked her head, still looking up at him. "You ever been married?"

"Once."

"What happened?"

"She left me."

"Did you cheat on her?"

He supposed, considering Annie's experiences, that was a logical question. It couldn't, however, have been further from the mark. "No, I was faithful."

"She cheated on you." Annie wrinkled her nose. "Bum deal."

"In a way, you could say she cheated on me. Cheated on our wedding vows. You know that part about promising to 'love and cherish until death do us part'? Well, my dear Marian left me because she found herself married to a man without any money." He waved his fingers in the air. "No money. Bye-bye."

He was making light of the situation, but Annie saw the pain in his eyes and knew he'd been hurt deeply. Still, she was confused. A glance around the room found the symbols of wealth everywhere. "How much money did she want?"

"Any, at that time, might have been good." Link followed her glance. "I haven't always had this. Actually, about seven years ago, my bank account was so far in the red, I was looking for a spot on the street to set up my cardboard box."

"And she couldn't take it?"

He shook his head. "Marian had a picture of how her

life would be. When we met, I fit into that picture. I was teaching at the college and bringing in a fair amount of money. She saw our lives as a series of academic parties, intellectual gatherings, and comfortable trips around the world. I screwed up her dream by deciding I wanted to invent things instead of teach. I quit my job and invested all of my money in the manufacturing of a garbage disposal I thought every woman would want."

He shook his head. "As I said, even certified geniuses can do dumb things. No one wanted my garbage disposal and a year later, not only was my money gone, I'd borrowed so much to pull this off, I was in hock up to my ears. That's when Marian left."

"Because you lost your money." Annie sensed there was more to the story.

"She took off like a rat leaving a sinking ship. Wouldn't even talk to me after that. Her lawyer handled everything."

"What about before? Did you talk to her before you quit your job and invested all of your money in that invention? Did you let her know your plans?"

He glanced over toward the window. "She had an idea of what I was doing."

"An idea?" Annie knew then what the problem was. She'd been right. "You sound just like my father and brother. When you're on the top, you know it all. You don't need a woman's advice or opinion, don't feel it's necessary to include her in your plans. But when something goes wrong, boy, oh, boy, if we're not there holding your hand, it's all our fault."

He glared down at her. "So you think Marian was right?"

"Not necessarily right, but I have a feeling she felt as wronged as you do."

"I should have known better than to think a woman would understand."

"Ah, but that's where you're wrong. I do understand. You said it yourself. She loved an image. You destroyed that image without asking her permission."

"So what image did my father destroy to give my mother reason to leave him and two small boys?"

That Annie didn't know. She only knew it had left her son with a chip on his shoulder. Pushing herself up to her feet, she stretched the kinks out of her body. "I think it's time to get you back into bed."

"Yeah." He looked at the bed, then at her.

She held out her hands. "Easy up, like we've done before."

He took her hands and she pulled him to his feet, his right leg bearing no weight. Positioning herself along his right side, she acted as a crutch, and he took the one step necessary to get him close to the bed. Then she helped him turn, so his back was facing the bed. She expected him to sit down. Instead, he slipped his arms around her shoulders, capturing her in an embrace.

"And what about you?" he asked, holding her there and looking down at her with those dark, velvety eyes. "Do you still believe in love and marriage?"

Annie's heart jumped to her throat as her stomach did a flip. She could feel the weight of his arms on her shoulders, feel the warmth of his body and the latent strength he possessed. He wasn't holding her tight; he didn't need to. The way he was looking at her, she couldn't have moved if she'd wanted to.

She also couldn't think, and she knew he was waiting for an answer to his question. Problem was, she could barely breathe, much less talk.

"Well?" he asked, his smile seductive.

"I—I think so."

"Why?"

"Because . . . because it happens." She forced the words to come. "Because we need it to happen. If people didn't fall in love and get married, after a while society would fail."

"So why not have arranged marriages? Let some bureaucracy figure out who should be matched with whom. Then those two people would have to stick together, no matter what."

"I don't want anyone telling me who I can fall in love with and marry."

"You're willing to trust luck?"

"I'd rather have the choice."

"And what if you choose the wrong person?"

She knew Link was the wrong person. That's why it bothered her that having his arms wrapped around her neck was having such an unnerving effect on her. "Link, we need to get you into bed."

He smiled, and she knew she hadn't disguised her reaction to him. The way her voice was quavering and her legs trembling, he'd have to be an idiot not to realize what he was doing to her. "Didn't you say," he asked, "that I needed to be on my feet more?"

"I meant on crutches." Not so close that she could feel the warmth of his breath on her forehead. In a minute she was going to melt into his arms.

"I think I like this." He smiled down at her.

She liked it, too, liked it too much. She had to do something, so she tried for humor. "I think you're pressing your luck."

He chuckled, the sound warm and throaty. It didn't help calm her pulse.

"Link." She could push him back, but she didn't want him hurting his side.

Again, he blew his breath across her forehead, stirring her bangs. "Your divorce was five years ago?"

"Yes." She cringed at how husky that one word sounded. She might as well be telling him he aroused her. Looking up at him, seeing his expression, she knew she *was* telling him. She also knew she wasn't the only one who was aroused. Again, she said his name. "This has got to stop."

He grinned and eased down onto the bed. The contact broken, Annie scooted away, afraid if he touched her again, she'd throw herself at him. Quickly she moved down toward the end of the bed and helped him shift his legs up and under the covers. Then she walked to his other side, pushing the table with his papers and the telephone closer to his bed. He levered the bed to a sitting position and watched her.

"Do you have a boyfriend?" he asked.

She paused in her fussing, looked at him, and considered lying, but only for a moment. "No. Just Ziggy."

"And Ziggy is—?"

She grinned, knowing her answer wasn't going to be what he expected. "A Siamese cat with an attitude."

"And that's it?"

"That's it." She stepped away from his bed. "Anything else you'd like to know?"

"When you're going to crawl into bed with me."

She choked, not expecting the question, then came back with as quick a response as she could muster. "When you can chase me around this room, we'll discuss it."

"Good." He smiled and pushed the button to lower the bed back down. "Then I've got two things to get better for: a fuel cell and a run around this room."

SIX

She was the kind of woman a man dreamed of, all legs, a provocative thrust of breasts, and the face of an angel. But when she looked at me with those big blue eyes of hers, then ran the tip of her tongue over her lips, dampening them into a warm invitation, I knew she was no angel.

—The Naked Angel

From the corner of his eye, Link watched Annie walk into the great room carrying a vase of flowers. She thought he was working on his notes, and he should be, but whenever she was around, his concentration switched to her.

Here it was, after nine o'clock at night, and she was still full of energy, puttering here and there. Straightening things. Arranging things.

Tempting him.

She was always on the move, sitting down only when she was reading one of her mysteries or working on one of those puzzles she liked. She didn't watch much television, which surprised him, and her tastes in music were eclectic, paralleling his if anything.

He wanted to ignore her—forget she was there—but that was impossible. How could you ignore eyes as blue as hers, eyes that revealed every emotion she experienced? Or a voice that could both excite and soothe?

He had never had problems concentrating on a project when a woman was around, not even when he was married. Now his mind kept drifting to things Annie had said or done, the cute way she wrinkled her nose when she didn't like something or the sound of her laughter, so light and spontaneous. He wanted to tell her to stay out of the great room, to stay far, far away from him, but he wouldn't. To admit that she bothered him would give her power, and she already had way too much power.

She placed the vase on the farthest end table from him, next to the sofa, and stepped back to look at the arrangement. She'd been going through the flowers he'd received while in the hospital and since, throwing away the dead blossoms and trimming the ends on those that could be salvaged. Stepping forward again, she shifted the vase slightly to the left, then, satisfied, picked up the paperback mystery she'd left on the sofa.

He knew the moment she looked his way.

"I'm going to take this up to my car and get a couple new books," she said, holding up the paperback.

"Sure, whatever," he said, trying to sound indifferent.

He watched her leave the room and smiled. Ever since he'd suggested she crawl into bed with him, an uneasy tension had hovered between them, almost a feeling of anticipation.

She was as efficient as ever in her nursing duties, and relentless in his physical therapy exercises. It was in their casual contact that he had noticed a difference. When she helped him out of bed, she made sure he couldn't get her in an embrace. And she kept their conversations on non-personal topics. She now knew as much about the grass fire that had whipped through the Oakland-Berkeley hills in '91 as he did. And he'd told her all about the automotive antitheft device he'd invented, along with the tracker now being used by police to recover stolen cars, and the robotics ignition shutdown system that ended high speed police chases and limited accidents. It was those inventions that had finally pulled his finances out of the red.

Annie was keeping their relationship on a professional basis, and Link knew he should do the same. Still, he wanted more. He liked it when he got her pulse racing, liked the flush in her cheeks and the look that darkened her eyes. And he liked how she made him feel. It had been a long time since he'd lusted for a woman. It was good to know he still could.

He wasn't worried that it was anything more than lust. His short-lived marriage had cured him of that sickness called love. What he wanted with Annie was simple. One word described it. Sex.

She turned him on, and he was pretty sure he was affecting her temperature gauge. Once his strength was back and he was out of this bed and on his feet for more than ten minutes, he was going to do exactly as he'd promised. Maybe not chase her around the room, but he was going to catch her. Considering the way she looked at him when she didn't think he was paying attention, he had a feeling "catching" her wasn't going to be too difficult.

Annie let herself out the front door and paused. The foyer she was in was still inside the building. In front of her was the elevator and to her right was a door that led to the outside and a flight of steps that went up the hill. Often she took the steps, just for the exercise, but it was dark outside and fog had crept up from the bay, clinging close to the ground. Through the window in the side door, she could see little but the misty haze and the diffused light of a distant house. Going up the stairs did not seem like a wise idea.

She took the elevator to the carport, and the moment she stepped out, she could hear the woeful sound of a distant foghorn. She glanced to her left, where normally a panorama of lights illuminated the city below. Tonight only an occasional glimmer pierced the thick blanket of fog. The gray mist, like the malevolent fingers on a ghostly hand, had silently crept up the hills and was now wrapping itself around everything in sight.

Behind her, the elevator door automatically closed, shutting off that source of light, and she wished she'd brought a flashlight. If she'd been smart, she would have come up earlier, before it got dark . . . before the fog had settled in. She'd thought about it once or twice, but each time she'd gotten distracted and had started a new project. It wasn't until a few minutes earlier, when she saw the book she'd finished that afternoon, that she'd remembered she didn't have anything to read when she went to bed.

A noise startled her, sounding like metal hitting cement. The clank sent an icy chill down her back that had nothing to do with the cold, misty air.

It came from the far side of the carport, over near Link's Jaguar. "Who's there?" she asked, taking a step back, closer to the elevator door.

She knew she could push the button and the door would open, but she didn't. An open elevator door would give her more light, but if someone was out there, that light would also make her more visible.

It was too dark.

She'd come up to her car this late before. It had never been this dark. A security light came on every night. Came on automatically once it got dark. It should be throwing some illumination over the carport, even in this fog.

A quick glance told her what she already knew. The light was out. The bulb had been broken.

Again, a foghorn blew in the distance, and she held her breath, listening for any other sounds. What she heard was the beating of her heart, and maybe something else, something moving. Then again, with her pulse thrumming in her ears, it was hard to tell.

"Is anyone out there?" she asked, knowing how foolish she was being.

Who was going to answer? A thief? Not likely.

She read mysteries. Watched them on television and in the movies. She was being as stupid as most of the victims in those stories. Here she was, standing around, just asking to be attacked. If she were wise, she would hightail it out of there and forget getting a book from her car. She would take the elevator back down and return to the safety of the house. Return to the safety of Link.

As if being around him was safe.

She took a step back, then a clamor down the street stopped her. The noise had sounded almost like the one she'd heard earlier. A dog started barking, then another took up the chorus, and Annie understood what was going on. That afternoon she'd set Link's garbage cans out. In front of each house in the neighborhood was at least one garbage can. Some houses had two or three. In the morning, the truck would be by. But meanwhile, the raccoons that lived in the canyon were having a field day. And if not them, there were opossums and skunks, as well as cats.

She changed her mind about going back down. She wasn't going to let a raccoon scare her off. After all, her car was only a few feet away. All she had to do was open the door, grab a couple of books, and she'd be out of there.

Just to be safe, however, she pulled Link's umbrella from the stand beside the elevator. She held it like a weapon, ready to poke or swing at anyone or anything that might run—or waddle—toward her. Armed and ready, she took a tentative step toward her car.

An outside light came on over at the house across the road, and a new voice joined the other barking dogs. Annie knew his name was Barney, that he was a three-year-old rottweiler, and that he barked at anything and everything that moved. She had a feeling he was barking at her and glanced that way. Through the fog, she could barely see the dog, but he was at the neighbor's chain-link fence, facing her direction.

Of course, he might be barking at something besides her, something or someone over near Link's car. Poised halfway between her car and the elevator, she debated that possibility.

It had to be her, she finally decided, and took the last few steps to her Geo. Her keys out, she slipped one into the lock and gave it a turn.

She stayed alert, watching for any shadowy movement that might catch her eye and listening for any sounds, though Barney's barking made that almost impossible. The light came on inside her car the moment she opened the door. She tossed the book she'd finished onto the backseat—it joined several others—and pulled two more from the box on the front seat.

Her last patient had given her the box of paperbacks. Some were new, but most were used; a collection of that patient's reading habits. Annie had brought the entire box, not sure which of the books she might have already read and what would be new. She now wondered if she shouldn't just bring the box into the house, and she might have if it had been in better condition. Its musty smell, however, was bad enough in her car. She didn't want it in her room. And there was another thought. The box would encumber her if someone did attack her.

The two books in hand, she closed her car door, locked it again, and took in a deep breath, glancing around. She still couldn't hear anything, not with the dog barking across the road. She also couldn't see anything, which was somewhat reassuring. She wasn't sure what she would do if someone did suddenly appear.

Reason told her she should check out the area, look around Link's car and hers. Reason also told her not to be an idiot and to get back into the house. She went with her second thought and made her way back to the elevator, constantly looking around. She didn't breathe easily until the elevator door opened, flooding light into the area. Only then did she drop the umbrella back into its rack. Once inside the elevator, she pushed the down button and the door closed. As the elevator started down, she sighed in relief.

Link heard the elevator descend and waited, listening for the front door to open, then close again. He pretended he was busy with his notes and didn't look up when Annie walked into the room. Only when she spoke did he turn his head her way.

"Your yard light's out up there," she said. "It's broken."

He saw the two books she held in her hand. He also noticed she seemed uneasy. "Afraid of the dark?" he asked, teasing.

"I heard something."

"What?" He dropped the teasing. He could tell she was concerned.

"I'm not sure. It sounded like something metallic dropping on the cement. Over by your car."

"Something metallic?"

She shrugged, but the concern was still there. "I'm

not sure. I heard another noise too. Farther down the street, then the dogs started barking, including that one across the road. I think what's happening is animals are getting into the garbage cans. Cats. Raccoons. Maybe even skunks."

He wouldn't disagree. "Raccoons are always coming up from the canyon and checking out the garbage cans."

"I know. You told me that. It was probably a raccoon."

"Did you look around?"

"It was dark. Your light's out."

She'd been scared. For some reason, Link found it comforting to know that the ever efficient Ms. Annie Marsden could be frightened by a raccoon. "I think you read too many of those mysteries. You're spooking yourself out. Seeing boogeymen where they don't exist."

"Well, it could have been someone," she argued, lifting her chin as she always did when she became defensive. "You've got an expensive car up there. Don't you worry about it? Worry that someone might steal it while you're down here?"

"It's equipped with an alarm—my alarm and locking system. No one's going to steal it. Besides, my neighbor's house is right across the road, their kitchen looks directly into my carport."

"It's foggy out. You can hardly see your hand in front of your face."

"So what do you want me to do? Call the police?"

"No." She shook her head. "I'm sure you're right. It was just a raccoon." She smiled halfheartedly. "They're out and about, and I'm ready to crash. Unless you need something more, I'm going to go to bed and read."

"So what are you reading tonight?" He didn't want her to leave. Not yet.

She glanced at the books in her hand. "Either Dick Francis or Mary Higgins Clark."

"You always read mysteries?"

"Most of the time. Why? Not intellectual enough in your opinion?"

He shrugged. "Just seems like you might want a change now and then."

"I sometimes read other things." Her tone was defensive. "Besides, a mystery isn't a mystery isn't a mystery. There are differences between authors. Different types of mysteries. Sometimes you know who the bad guy is and it's just a matter of following how the lead character discovers who it is. Sometimes you don't know who did it, not until the very end, and it's fun to try and guess."

He could tell she was relaxing. Some of the tension was gone from her posture, and she'd stepped closer, whether she realized it or not.

"With Mary Higgins Clark," she went on, "I've gotten so I know it's the one I least suspect. With Dick Francis, I like the way he tells the story, and of course, his always have something to do with horses. He was a steeplechase jockey, you know."

"So when are you going to write a mystery?"

She laughed, the sound light and easy. "Probably right after I become a doctor."

"So why not? Be a doctor. Be a writer. Do whatever you want to do."

She rubbed the thumb and forefingers of one hand together. "There's a little thing called money. I still owe on a college loan, and I do like to eat occasionally."

"Sometimes you've just got to follow your dreams."

"Like you've done?" She looked around. "It would be nice to have a dream turn out like this." She turned back to him and grinned. "Maybe someday you'll walk into a bookstore and buy a mystery written by Dr. Annie Marsden."

"Why not?"

"Why not indeed?"

"I'll tell everyone I slept with her."

She opened her mouth in surprise, then started to laugh. "Oh, you will, will you? Well, don't forget, you have to catch me first."

"Anytime you're ready."

"I hope you have your running shoes on." She walked down to the end of his bed and pulled the covers over the exposed toes of his broken leg.

"Are you fussing again?" he asked, watching her.

"Yes." She tapped him on his cast, the sound hollow. "Are you grumbling again?"

"Maybe."

"Good. I wouldn't know what to do if you didn't." She glanced at the pad of paper he'd been working on. "Don't stay up too late."

She started to walk off, but he called to her. "What, no good-night kiss?"

Without stopping, she called back her answer. "In your dreams, Dr. Sheffield. In your dreams."

Link watched her leave the room and listened as she went down the stairs. She was right. If tonight was like last night and the night before, he would be kissing her in his dreams. Kissing her and doing a heck of a lot more. His body was definitely healing.

SEVEN

I watched the couples gyrating on the pint-sized square that the Sea Breeze called a dance floor. Tommy was at the bar, his back to me, talking to a blond babe who seemed to be hanging on to his every word. I knew Tommy wasn't on this cruise to meet women. What I needed to do was get closer, listen in on what he was saying. I adjusted my balance to the sway of the ship and started toward him.

—Cruise to Crime

"Easy," Annie said. "Stop and rest a minute."

Link swayed on his crutches, a slight sheen of perspiration dampening his forehead. It was the first time he'd gone down and then back up the stairs. And, of course, he had to do it all at one time, had to prove he could. How like a man, Annie thought. He turned everything into a challenge.

"I'm fine," he said, pausing at the top of the steps, his breathing ragged.

"Yeah, right." Annie stayed close beside him. She didn't want him passing out and falling back down the stairs. She was strong, but a hundred seventy pounds, give or take a few, was more than she wanted to catch. "You want to head for the sofa or your bed?"

"Sofa," he said, and took a step in that direction. "I can't believe . . . I'm this"—he was breathing hard and swaying slightly as he swung his crutches over the carpeting—"out of shape."

"What? You thought you could bounce out of bed and run the marathon?" She stayed close, ready to help if necessary. "Just think how weak you would be if I hadn't been forcing you to do those exercises. How's your side feeling?"

"Okay."

"You know, it's not a weakness to admit pain." She'd seen him grimace more than once when he started to go off balance. "Cut and torn muscles don't heal overnight, or even in a week."

"I am fine," he said through clenched teeth.

"I'm sorry, I forgot. You're Mr. Macho, aren't you? Two more steps." She gauged the distance to the sofa as more like four steps, but what the heck, she'd lied to patients before. She preferred to think of it as stretching the truth.

She expected him to collapse onto the sofa as soon as he reached it. Instead, he stopped beside it and, leaning on his crutches, looked at her. "What?" she asked, uncomfortable with the way he was smiling.

"I need help."

"Help?" For him to ask for her help was unusual. "Doing what?"

"Help me turn around so my back is toward the sofa."

His request didn't make sense. He'd turned himself around on crutches before. Still, she couldn't very well refuse to help him, not after chastising him for playing Mr. Macho. "Okay." She stepped in front of him, put one hand on his left arm, and reached for his right. "Shift your weight to your left and move your right crutch, then ease yourself around so your back is to the sofa."

She stayed in front of him as he moved, so if he did lose his balance, she could stop him from falling on his face. She was getting so she liked the way he looked, his bruises and cuts well on their way to fading into nothing. Though not exactly handsome, he had an intriguing face. No need to add any new scars to it.

He made the turn easily, but still didn't sit on the sofa. She frowned her confusion. He answered her with a question. "Do you know what will happen if I fall forward?"

"You'll land on your face."

"No. I'll land on you."

"You're assuming I wouldn't step away and let you fall on your face."

He leaned slightly forward, and she knew he was testing her. To compensate for his change in balance, she gripped his arms tighter, pushing back. His gaze dropped down to her lab coat and the scooped-neck red top she had on, and she realized where he was looking. "Behave yourself," she ordered, and arched her back to hold him upright as he tilted closer to her.

"I'm doing what you tell me to do all the time," he

said, swaying ever so slightly so she had to keep readjusting her balance.

"And what is it I keep telling you to do?" Annie was tempted to step away and let him fall. It would serve him right.

"I'm keeping my muscles limber."

"I would think your trek up and down those stairs would have been exercise enough."

He smiled. "This is one specific muscle. Do you realize you have a very seductive mouth?"

The way he was looking at her, and the tone of his voice, sent a shiver of anticipation down her spine. "Link Sheffield, if you don't stop this, I'm just going to walk away."

"You wouldn't."

"I wouldn't bet on it."

"I would."

The way he said those two words—so softly and seductively—she knew she wouldn't. "Link, please. Sit down."

"What's the matter, Annie? Don't you like holding me in your arms?"

"I am not holding you in my arms." She pushed a little harder, hoping to force him off balance so he would fall back onto the sofa. "I think there must be something in that medicine you're taking that's affecting you."

"You mean it's not your perfume?"

Not the least bit bothered by her efforts to unbalance him, he leaned his head down, taking a sniff, and Annie wished she hadn't put perfume on that morning. It was a habit with her. One she would have to remember to break.

Link blew out his breath, and she felt the warmth of it slide down her bare throat and under the neckline of her top. Her stomach muscles tightened, and she swallowed hard. Then he blew into her hair, and she knew she had to stop him, stop what was happening. The verbal teasing was becoming a reality, and the idea of him chasing her around the room for a kiss didn't seem as far-fetched as it had been two days ago. Worst of all, the idea was beginning to sound tempting.

"Link, sit down," she ordered, using her sternest voice.

Almost as if acting as an exclamation point, the doorbell rang. Both Link and Annie looked in that direction, then at each other. "Who would that be?" he asked.

She'd been about to ask the same question and merely shook her head. Whoever it was, was a lifesaver. She felt Link lean back, his weight shifting off her. Then he eased himself down onto the sofa with the exhaling of a breath, and let the crutches fall where they might.

"I'll go see who it is," Annie said. She stepped back, glancing at him, then leaned forward and pulled his robe together, belting it at the waist. "Got to have you looking respectable," she said, then again stepped back.

Link knew what she meant, knew what she'd seen when she'd glanced at his hips. There was a most definite bulge in his pajama bottoms that needed to be covered; a part of his anatomy that needed to be tamed, controlled . . . or, better yet, satisfied. She'd seen him naked often enough, and she'd seen him with a hard-on most of the time. There was something about her near-ness that kept him in that condition. Be it her perfume or simply her presence, she could arouse him with the small-est of smiles or the lightest of touches. Falling on top of her might have been awkward. Falling into her would be better.

He watched her walk out of the room to answer the door. Her lab coat covered the seat of her jean shorts, but he could still see a little wiggle. He could also see part of a stethoscope hanging out of one pocket and a rectangular bulge in the other pocket, where he knew she kept the paperback mystery she was reading that particular day.

She was a mystery to him. Or maybe the mystery was his reaction to her. He didn't understand why the thought of kissing her had taken on such monumental proportions. She was just a woman. Cute, to be sure. Sexy, in her own way. But certainly not extraordinarily beautiful or alluring. Maybe she was right, maybe it was something in his medicine that was making him react this way. He'd heard that the medicine prescribed for Parkin-son's disease had an aphrodisiac effect. He'd have to call his doctor and ask him about his prescriptions.

He heard Annie open the door and offer a greeting. Then he heard another voice, one he recognized immedi-ately. His lab assistant was back from her cruise, and from the frantic tone of Diane's voice, she was almost in hys-terics. Link prepared himself, making sure his robe cov-ered his pajamas and that he was sitting up straight, not slumping. He didn't want her simpering over him, fussing and worrying. Annie did that well enough. Not the sim-pering, but the fussing.

Diane burst into the room with a rush of apologies. "I just heard this morning," she exclaimed. "Dan Zura called. I couldn't believe it. There I was, on that cruise, having fun in the sun, and you were nearly killed. Oh, my gosh."

She stopped in front of the sofa, and he knew from Diane's expression that no matter what Annie said, he didn't look great. Actually, he saw his face every morning when he shaved. After a while, you got used to looking at skin that had a purple and yellow tinge. Obviously, it would take Diane a while.

"Oh, my gosh, Professor Sheffield," she groaned, and her glance went down to the leg with a cast. "Oh, my gosh."

He was already getting tired of her fussing. "I'm fine, Diane. A little bruised and battered, but fine."

"If I had known." Tears started sliding down her cheeks and she shook her head, sniffling. "There I was, having fun and—and . . ."

He wasn't sure what to do. His box of tissues was over near his bed, and he glanced that way. Annie had already picked up the box and was walking toward Diane. "Here," she said, handing the tissue box to Diane. "I'll get you a chair."

She pushed one of the easy chairs over so Diane could sit in front of him. In his opinion, he didn't need his assistant that close, but he said nothing. "Can I get you something to drink?" Annie asked them both.

"Oh, no . . . no, nothing," Diane said, her gaze never leaving his face.

Link shook his head. "What I want," he said to Annie,

"is for you to sit down." He patted the cushion next to him.

For a moment, he thought she might object, or at least sit somewhere else. It would be like her. To his surprise, she glanced at Diane, then at him, then did exactly as he'd asked and sat down next to him. Without realizing he'd been holding his breath, he let it out. "I gather you two met at the door."

"Yes," Diane said right away. "She said she's your nurse. I've had some nursing experience. I could—"

"There's something I need to explain," Link interrupted. "Annie's more than my nurse."

Diane's gaze shot to Annie, and Link saw Annie frown. "What he means is—" she began.

He shook his head, stopping her. "Diane understands what I mean, honey. We need to let her know I'm well taken care of. I don't want her worrying about me."

He hoped Annie caught on. There was only so much he could explain.

When she smiled and nodded, then leaned back against the sofa, he knew she would play along. He turned to Diane. "So how was your cruise? You said you had fun?"

Diane's gaze jumped from Link to Annie, then back to him. He knew she had a crush on him. Perhaps he should have been flattered. Diane was a sweet person, and not unattractive. In fact, she had pretty brown hair and eyes. Her problem was she was emotionally immature. Possibly because she was a little overweight and hadn't dated a lot. She was also a romantic, and he wouldn't put it past her to see his situation now as an opportunity to win his heart. So maybe what he'd just done was cruel, but allowing her to think she had a chance, or that he returned her feelings, would have been even crueler.

"My cruise," she finally said. "Yes, it was fun. Wonderful. A whole week of relaxation and marvelous food. I'm glad I went, but—I saw the lab. I drove over there before I came here."

"It's a total wreck from what I've heard."

Diane nodded. "From the front, it doesn't look too bad. I mean, the building is still standing, and other than broken windows, it looks like it usually does. But I parked and got out." She shook her head. "I couldn't go in, they have it sealed off, but when I walked around to the side, where the trash bins are . . . were . . . I couldn't believe my eyes. What a mess. And to think you were in there when it happened." Again, she shook her head. "Dan said it happened at night, that you'd just stepped into the room and bam." She gestured with her hands. "From what was left of the lab, I—I wasn't sure how you would look."

"I guess I was lucky." Though at the time he hadn't felt lucky.

Annie leaned toward Diane. "You left the same day as the explosion. Is that right?"

Diane nodded, her attention switching to Annie. "Yes. We left that morning. Mom and I caught a plane from San Francisco to Fort Lauderdale." She paused and explained. "Mom went on the cruise with me. I won a cruise for two, so I asked her."

"That was nice of you," Annie said. "Tell me, though, did you go into the lab at all that day?"

"No. Mom spent the night before with me and we just got up and drove to the airport." Diane looked at Link, clearly confused. "Why?"

He smiled reassuringly. "You'll have to get used to Annie," he said, and slipped an arm along the back of the sofa behind Annie's head. He did it for effect, but he also did it for himself. He was getting used to her, and he was definitely enjoying having her seated next to him.

"Besides being a nurse," he went on, "Annie sees herself as a detective. It comes from all the mysteries she reads. Thing is, she thinks someone planted a bomb in my lab."

Diane gasped. "And you think I did it?"

"No," Annie said quickly. "I'm just trying to put the pieces together. You saw the lab just a while ago. From what you saw, could you tell where the explosion occurred?"

"Not really. Just that it was near the area where we always worked, where Link . . . Professor Sheffield had the prototype."

"And the last time you were there, was there anything in that area that might have blown up? By accident, I mean."

"No." Diane looked back at Link. "I can't think of anything that might have blown up on its own. I mean, I did have that can of spray for static cling in my desk. I think it might explode if you tossed it into a fire. I don't know."

"This was no can of spray exploding," Link said. That night might be hazy in his mind, but he knew the difference.

"How about gas valves?" Annie went on. "Ever have any problems with gas leaks?"

Again, Diane looked at him, her uncertainty obvious. "I don't think so."

"No," he said. "Besides, I've been thinking about that possibility. If the explosion had occurred when I turned on the light, it could be plausible that a spark caused the explosion. But I remember turning on the light and walking toward the fuel cell. Too much time passed between the two events."

Annie grimaced and sighed. "Then, other than assuming someone planted a bomb, something set with a timer, I can't think of anything else that might have caused that explosion." Almost immediately, she turned back to Diane. "Had you been planning this cruise for a long time?"

"Heavens no," she said. "It was a big surprise to me. I didn't even remember entering the contest, though I do enter a lot of contests." She looked at Link and grinned. "You never know when you might get lucky. Gotta chase the dream."

Link knew that was what he was always saying when he tried something new. He couldn't argue. "You're right."

"Was there any particular reason why you chose last week to go?" Annie asked, bringing the conversation back to the point.

Diane nodded. "Spring break. I had to take the trip within four weeks or forfeit it, and with finals coming up soon, this was the best time."

"You had only a month in which to claim your prize?"

Link could see the wheels turning in Annie's head. She had missed her calling. She should be doing detective work.

"That's what *they* said."

" 'They' being the contest officials, I assume. Didn't that seem strange?"

"I don't know. It all seemed a little strange." She looked at Link. "Remember me saying that?"

He remembered. At the time, however, he hadn't cared. He'd simply been angry because she was going to be gone for a week. Still he could see what Annie was getting at. "You think her winning that trip has something to do with the explosion?"

"I don't know. It just seems like a big coincidence. She wins a cruise, but doesn't remember entering the contest. She has to take the trip within a very short time, just when you're nearing spring break. And the night after she leaves, your lab blows up."

"But I didn't do it," Diane said, her voice cracking.

"I'm not saying you did," Annie insisted. "But I think someone wanted you gone."

"But why?"

"Good question."

There were lots of good questions, Link mused. The problem was, they didn't have any good answers. None of them. After a while, the subject was dropped. Diane gave a brief rundown of her trip, Link assured her he'd keep paying her salary—he knew she needed the money for school—and he encouraged her to put her efforts into her studies, then promised to call her once he decided what he was going to do about another prototype. For one thing, he told her, he needed a new workplace. They couldn't use the old lab, and he didn't want to work at his house. The place just wasn't designed for a project of that nature. Dan would have to scout up a building they could rent and get the necessary equipment. Then Diane could start helping again.

"I'll call you once I know what I'm doing," he repeated before Diane left, and she promised she'd be ready to help, anytime.

That night, after giving Link his final pill and putting everything away in the kitchen, Annie stepped into the great room to see if he was ready to go to bed. She found him leaning on his crutches in front of his picture window, watching the tail end of the evening's sunset. He'd changed out of his pajamas after Diane's visit, into a white T-shirt and gray sweats, but he still had on his blue robe. He was not quite the helpless victim she'd met six days earlier, nor was he fully recovered, but soon the hospital bed would be taken back to the rental company and her presence would no longer be needed. She hated to admit she was going to miss him.

As if sensing her presence, he glanced her way, then back out the window. "Have you seen what the fog's doing tonight?"

"No." She walked over to stand beside him and let her gaze travel from the stars that were making their presence known to the brilliant lights of the Oakland–San Francisco skyline and the Bay Bridge. It was beyond the city, just off the coastline where the sky still held a tinge of color, that a wall of fog lay like a theatrical backdrop. Thick and gray, it blotted out everything beyond, and it was poised to swallow up the city, held at bay only by the wind. "Weird," she said. "It has sort of a spooky look to it."

"Perfect setting for a mystery, don't you think?"

She looked up at him and saw he was smiling. "Are you trying to make fun of me, Dr. Sheffield?"

"Now, would I do that?"

She knew he would. "Yes."

"Maybe you've just taught me to think of everything in terms of a mystery. What did you think of Diane?"

His change of topic took her off guard. Annie shrugged. "I don't know. You were right. She's very young-acting for her age. Probably very smart, but not too sophisticated. I think she has a crush on you."

"Of course she has a crush on me, and it's darn irritating."

She laughed at his exasperated tone. "I bet you were always grumbling at her when you were working together. I can't say I appreciate your implying more is going on between us than my being your nurse."

"Call it wishful thinking. And it should keep her from coming back and fussing over me."

"You and your fussing."

He grunted.

"Why are you so against being fussed over? Most men love it."

"Well good. You women who want to fuss should go fuss over them." He looked away, back out at the skyline.

"My grandmother fussed. When I was little, she fussed all the time."

"That's what grandmothers are supposed to do."

He wrinkled his nose. "She had bad breath."

"Well, I don't have bad breath. At least, I hope I don't."

"You sure?" he asked, looking back down at her.

"Do I?" She grimaced and tried to remember when she'd last brushed her teeth.

"I think we need to check."

She should have understood what he meant by that and where the conversation was headed. She should have stepped back. Instead, she stood where she was, looking up at him, her lips parting as she asked, "What?"

Using his crutches to keep his balance, Link reached out and caught her by the shoulders, drawing her closer. And he used her parted lips to convey his answer. As he kissed her, his mouth covering hers with firm assurance, the touch of his lips sent a shock of excitement clear through her. Like a bolt of lightning, it stood the hairs on the back of her neck on end and sapped her strength, her knees going weak.

She knew she had to stop him. A nurse didn't kiss her patient. Not like this. Maybe a peck on the cheek, but not a full-fledged, tongue-in-the-mouth, earthshaking, heart-stopping kiss.

She put her hands on his chest, but instead of pushing him away, her fingers curled into the soft fabric of his robe and held on. Instead of stopping the kiss, she moved her mouth with his, tasting and experiencing, forgetting all of the things a nurse shouldn't do. Shoulds and should nots turned to likes and wants. Most of all, Annie didn't want him to stop.

He teased her into stepping closer, and he tempted her into responding. Each thrust of his tongue created all sorts of images in her head and brought about an involuntary tightening of the muscles between her legs.

He was no longer the fallen warrior, wounded in battle. He was on his feet, seducing her, and she was succumbing without a fight. No fussing was his rule, and she certainly wasn't making a fuss now.

The kiss went on and on, until a need to breathe forced them to take a break. Stunned, she leaned against him, and he nuzzled the side of her face. "Caught you," he said in a low husky voice.

It took a moment for the words to register, then she pulled back and looked at him. "This is all a game to you, isn't it?"

And like a fool, she'd played along.

"No. No game. Believe me, I am very serious." He glanced toward his hospital bed. "I want to make love with you."

She repeated his words, turning them into a question. "You want to make love with me?"

"Yes. Tonight. Now. But maybe we'd better go downstairs, use my bed down there."

"You want to make love. Tonight. Now."

She stared at him, thinking how much he sounded like her ex. Dennis had approached lovemaking the same way. *Now. Here.* He'd treated her like an object, and she'd let him. Well, she wasn't going to allow that to happen again. "No," Annie said. Shaking her head, she stepped away.

Link's frown was fierce. "Are you going to tell me you don't want to do it? That you don't feel anything?"

"It doesn't matter what I want or feel," she said, angry with herself for being so transparent that he knew how he affected her. "You men. All you think about is sex. That and proving who's better than the other. Well, I'm sorry. If you want a quick roll in the hay, you're going to have to call up one of your lady friends."

"I don't have any 'lady friends' to call up. And I'm not talking about a quick roll in the hay."

"Oh, yeah? You're saying this is going to be a long-term relationship? That you're going to call me up after I leave this job? That we'll make a date? Go out?"

"Maybe."

"Well good." She knew he wouldn't call. "After I'm off this assignment, you give me a call, and we'll continue this conversation. Until then, I don't sleep with my patients. Good night."

She turned and walked away. If he was well enough to try to seduce her, he was well enough to get himself to bed. In fact, in Annie's opinion, Link Sheffield could do all sorts of things by himself that night.

"You don't, you know," he said.

She stopped and looked back, frowning. "I don't what?"

"Have bad breath."

EIGHT

"Darling, you're driving too fast!"

"I'm not the one who's driving too fast. I'm simply trying to keep up with him. He's the one who's driving too fast."

"Remember the time you ran the Desoto into a tree?"

"That wasn't my fault, dear. You know that. I had to swerve to miss that dog."

—The Case of the Hairpin Turn

"Time to get out of here." Annie checked her watch. "If we leave now, we should make it to the doctor's by ten o'clock."

She grabbed her purse and hurried to the front door so she could hold it open for Link. In the last three days, he had gained back much of his strength and was getting so he could do most things on his own, but opening a door and pulling it closed took some maneuvering on crutches and they were running late.

Once Link had this checkup by the doctor, Annie was

sure she'd be out of a job. Gone was the bruised and battered patient she'd met the first day she'd arrived at this house. Link was quite capable of caring for himself now, though he wouldn't be able to drive until he got a walking cast on. Keeping a live-in nurse around just to act as a chauffeur, however, was a bit ridiculous when he could always call a cab.

She liked it when a patient got better, yet she knew she was going to miss Link's sexy teasing and their constant bantering. He didn't know how tempted she'd been that night he'd kissed her and asked her to share his bed, and since she was sure he wouldn't call her after she left, he would never know.

She watched him come toward her, swinging easily on his crutches, his smile seductively warm, and for a moment she regretted her decision not to make love with him. She knew, without a doubt, it would have been an experience she'd never forget.

Link swung past her and pushed the button for the elevator door. Immediately the door opened and he motioned for her to go in. "Ladies first."

She went to the far corner so he would have ample room to turn around. As the door slid closed, she glanced into the mirror by the control panel. She hadn't taken time to check her appearance before leaving the house.

Since they were going to the doctor's office, she'd put on a pair of white jeans, a white blouse, and her white lab coat. It was her closest concession to a uniform. She noticed her hair needed a trim, that her bangs were getting much too long, and she decided she'd have to make an appointment to get a haircut once this assignment was over.

Glancing Link's way, she smiled. He was the one who needed a haircut. Before they'd left, she'd tried to give him a trim. He'd said she was fussing and if the doctor didn't like the length of his hair, that was the doctor's problem. After ten days of living with Link, she knew she'd be wasting her time arguing and let it go at that.

The elevator jerked to a stop and the door slid open. The moment they stepped out, she started for her Geo. Before she'd taken two steps, Link stopped her. "I am not riding in that death trap. We're taking my car."

She looked over the top of her car toward his Jaguar, then back at him. "You want me to drive your car?"

"I'm sure not going in yours."

"I've never driven a Jag."

"So? It's a car. Fully automatic. You shouldn't have any problems."

Annie could think of all sorts of problems. She knew the feel of her car, how much gas to give it to accelerate to the speed she wanted, and how long it took to come to a full stop. She didn't know his car, and the idea of driving it petrified her. "How much did your car cost? Fifty, sixty thousand dollars?"

"Somewhere around there."

She knew from his grin it was more. "And if I get a ding in it?"

"You're not going to get a ding in it." He started toward his car, totally ignoring her.

"Your keys are downstairs. I'd have to go back down and get them. We'll be—"

She stopped. He'd pulled a set of keys from his shorts pocket. After showing them to her, he continued his journey.

She tried another angle. "I've never driven a car with that much power. My Geo is a stick shift. Seventy-five is top speed for me."

"I doubt we'll go over thirty-five or forty today," he said, and pushed something on the key. She heard the car's doors unlock and knew the antitheft device he'd invented had also been disarmed with that maneuver.

"If I put a ding in it, it's not my fault," she muttered. She held his crutches until he was seated on the passenger's side, then slipped the crutches behind him, so they rested on the backseat.

"You're not going to put a ding in it," he said, looking up at her. "You're going to love it. Now, just get in and drive."

Link could hear her grumbling all the way around the car, and smiled to himself. Most women he knew would die to be allowed to drive his car. In fact, he'd had complete strangers come up and ask if they could take it for a spin. But not Annie. No, she'd rather drive a Geo Metro, a car that looked more like one of the electric vehicles he'd been experimenting on than a "real" car.

She was a strange one.

So why was he attracted to her? he wondered. Why had that kiss the other night left him wanting more?

He didn't like it. He didn't want to be attracted to her, didn't want to have these feelings of desire. Every time she was near, he felt out of sorts. Irritable and edgy. He couldn't concentrate on his fuel cell. He couldn't ignore her and he couldn't forget how good her body had felt pressed against his. Every time he closed his eyes, the images would come back. Just thinking about it made him want her, and he didn't want to want her.

Annie slid into the driver's seat and stared open-mouthed at the white-on-black instruments in the wood panel that spanned the full width of the dashboard. "Here," he said sharply, handing her the key. He knew it wasn't right to take his frustration out on her, but he couldn't seem to help himself. From the first time he looked at her, he'd known she was going to be trouble. He should have let her go when he had the chance.

She put the key into the ignition and turned it. He saw her tense and give a start when the engine turned over. Link smiled and leaned back against the leather seat. He liked the sound of that much power. The XK8 was his baby, his reward for suffering through those years of poverty . . . for being deserted by a wife who didn't believe in him.

Annie drew in a deep breath, her hands resting on the wood and leather steering wheel, then she sighed and shifted into reverse. She stepped on the gas, and the car jumped back. Immediately she slammed on the brakes, bringing them to a jarring halt and throwing him forward so he had to brace his hands against the dash to keep from going into it. "What are you doing?" he snapped.

"I didn't expect it to—to—" She took in a deep breath and glared at him. "If you're going to make me drive this thing, I'd suggest you put on your seat belt."

He certainly would. "And I'd suggest you go easy on

that gas pedal. This car goes from zero to sixty in six point nine seconds."

"I'll remember that." She put her own seat belt on and checked behind her for traffic before again giving the car gas. There was a slight jerk, not as abrupt as the first time, and she didn't slam on the brakes but eased up on the gas until the car was inching back onto the street.

Once she'd gone far enough, she shifted into drive and turned the wheel so they were heading down Skyline Drive. Again, she gave the car gas, very slowly, and they started forward. Her fingers gripped the steering wheel like iron vises and her entire body was tense, reminding Link of the first time he'd driven a car—his dad's car. "Relax," he said. She looked like a prisoner on her way to the gas chamber.

She licked her lips, and gave him just the briefest of glances. "Easy for you to say."

"Hey, if anyone should be nervous, it should be me."

"Just remember, this was your idea."

"You should be enjoying this. Driving this car is like having sex."

"Leave it to a man to use sex as an analogy for driving a car."

He grinned. "I could say you're as tense as a virgin on her wedding night."

"You could, but you won't. Will you?"

She gave him another quick, wry smile, and he laughed. "I could also say, at the speed we're going, it will be late afternoon before we reach the bottom of the hill, much less the doctor's office. You can go a *little* faster, you know."

She checked the speedometer, then looked back out at the road. He felt the car pick up speed. They came to a curve, and she made a nice tight turn. The car picked up a little more speed, and she made the next turn a bit wider. A car passed them, going up the hill. He watched it go by, then looked ahead. She'd taken him too literally, he decided. She'd definitely increased their speed. In fact, she was now going too fast, certainly too fast for the next curve.

"Better put on the brakes," he said, feeling like a driving instructor.

"I am," she said, her voice tense and her eyes focused straight ahead. "I have been."

"Slow down," he ordered when the car went even faster instead of slowing.

"I can't, I'm telling you."

"What do you mean you can't?" She made the turn, but only by going into the other lane.

"Your brakes aren't working."

"Not working?" Her knuckles were white, her words clipped, and he could see she was pumping the brake and struggling to keep the car under control. "They're antilock brakes. You're not supposed to pump them."

They whipped around another curve, barely missing an oncoming car. "Then you tell me what to do," she said desperately. "Stepping on them didn't work. Pumping them isn't working. Damn!" She swerved to miss a rock in the road. "We keep picking up speed, and—" She flew past another car going up the hill. "I'm not sure how much longer I can keep this thing on the road, or what I'll do if—Oh, no."

Link looked ahead and knew what the problem was. They were coming up on another car going down the hill. Coming up fast.

He now wished they were in a car with a stick shift. That would have made things a little easier. With an automatic, he only had one option. "I'm going to put on the emergency brake," he said, trying to keep his voice calm. He didn't need her panicking. "I'm going to put it on slowly. You're going to feel the car pull to the side. Don't try to go around that car. If you do, chances are we'll go off the road and over the side into the canyon. Head for your right. Try to go up a driveway or something."

He pulled on the emergency brake. Slowly, so he wouldn't put them into a spin, but steadily. There was resistance to his pull, and his muscles also resisted, still not fully back to normal. He could feel the car dip down in front, and next to him Annie was fighting the wheel, trying to keep control. She steered for a driveway ahead and to the right. It angled uphill to a house, and he knew if they made it, gravity would bring the car to a stop. Gravity could be your enemy or your friend.

He felt the car begin to skid and was afraid it might go out of control. "Now!" he yelled. "Steer for that drive."

She yanked the wheel to the right, and he reached across the console to help. The car headed toward the driveway, sliding to the side. They were going too far to the right, and he pushed the wheel in the opposite direction to compensate, then pulled back again. The front wheels hit the cement of the drive, and he helped her spin the steering wheel to straighten the tires. But the car kept sliding to the side as well as traveling forward, and he heard the crunch of metal as the rear end wiped out the mailbox standing by the driveway.

"Oh, no," Annie groaned, and he saw a tree fill the windshield.

The next thing he knew the air bag was exploding, slamming into him like a concrete wall and knocking the breath out of his lungs. And then the car came to a stop.

A dead stop.

The air bag deflated as quickly as it had inflated, and Link turned toward Annie. She appeared to be all right. He could tell she was breathing. And as far as he could see, there was no blood. Still, she wasn't moving, she was just sitting there, staring at the deflated air bag in front of her. Rigidly staring.

"Annie, look at me," he demanded, frightened by her frozen appearance.

Slowly, she turned her head and looked at him, her eyes brimming with tears.

"Are you all right?"

"I—Yes, I think so."

With a sigh, she closed her eyes, and he saw the tears slide down her cheeks.

Link used his cell phone to call 911. The police arrived first, then an ambulance. Annie insisted she was fine—shaken but fine. The police, in turn, insisted she ride in the ambulance with Link and get a complete checkup. His doctor met them at the hospital. Two hours later, they were both released. The accident had caused no major injuries to either of them, but Link's doctor had suggested they both take it easy for the next twenty-four hours. He'd asked Annie to stay on the job another day or two, just to make sure Link was all right. She had a feeling, when the doctor asked to speak to Link privately, that he suggested Link keep an eye on her.

Annie was pretty sure Link couldn't care less about her well-being, considering what she'd done to his car. Well, he couldn't say she'd put a ding in it. When she did a job, she did a job well.

They took a taxi back to his house. Neither said much. There was nothing to say. She knew Link blamed her for the accident. In a way, she blamed herself, yet she knew she wasn't at fault. She hadn't caused those brakes to fail. She'd had no choice about hitting that tree.

A gray sedan was waiting for them at Link's house. The man who got out was in his forties, losing his hair, short in stature, and way overweight. The brown suit he was wearing was rumpled and not a good fit. Link introduced him as Detective Bronson, and Annie liked him immediately. His smile was warm and friendly and his handshake firm.

He rode the elevator down with them, waiting until Link was seated on the sofa before getting down to the reason for his visit, though all of them knew why the detective was there. "About your accident this morning," he began.

"I seem to be involved in a lot of accidents lately," Link said with a sigh, and Annie knew he was tired.

"So it would seem." Detective Bronson looked at her. "You've been with him since the explosion?"

"Since he came home from the hospital after the explosion," she corrected.

"Anything strange happen since then?"

"Strange?"

Both Link and Annie asked the question at the same time, then looked at each other.

"Threatening phone calls? Letters?"

"No," Link answered. "Why?"

"Well, your accidents aren't accidents," Detective Bronson said. "We know it was a bomb that caused the explosion in your lab. From what we can figure, it was in a briefcase by your assistant's work area. We've sent everything we have to the Bureau of Alcohol, Tobacco and Firearms. They'll run tests to determine if the bomb fits any patterns on record and to analyze its components. As for your car—"

He looked directly at her. "You were driving?"

"Yes," Annie said.

"It's a bit difficult with this," Link said, lifting his cast to make his point.

"When you first started down the hill, did you have brakes?"

"Yes. That is, I think I did." Annie tried to remember. "I know I used the brakes when I backed up. And they worked fine."

"She nearly threw me through the window," Link said.

Detective Bronson pulled out a small notebook and penciled in a notation. "So the brakes were working when you backed up. What about when you started down the hill?"

"You mean when I first started down the hill?" She wasn't sure if she understood.

"Maybe I should rephrase that question. When did you first realize you didn't have any brakes?"

That she remembered. Clearly. "It was after I picked up speed. We were coming to a curve. I felt I was going too fast, so I stepped on the brake. But nothing happened. So I stepped on it again. I mean, I know you're not supposed to pump antilock brakes, but these weren't doing anything."

"So you had brakes when you backed the car out of the carport, but as you were going down the hill, when you stepped on the brakes, you didn't feel you had anything. Is that right?"

"That's about it." She sat down on the sofa, next to Link. Saying it aloud helped ease the feelings of guilt. She looked at Link. "Honest, I tried to stop the car."

"I know." He took her hand in his, giving her fingers a squeeze. "You did everything you could . . . everything I would have done."

"Well, if it helps," Detective Bronson said, interrupting them, "those brakes had been tampered with. You probably had just enough brake fluid left in the lines to stop the car that first time. After that, you might as well have opened the car door and dragged your foot along the pavement."

"Someone cut my brake line?" Link frowned his confusion.

"That's the way it looks. Nice neat job too. If you'd been in a crash, we might not have noticed, might have thought it was a result of the accident."

"That night—" Annie began, and looked at Link.

Detective Bronson's sharp gaze focused on her. "What night?"

Annie looked back at him. "A few nights ago, I went up to get some books out of my car. It was late and very foggy. The security light up there was out. The bulb was broken. And right after I stepped out of the elevator, I heard a noise, a clang or something, over near Link's car."

"Did you go investigate this noise?" Bronson asked.

"No." Now she wished she had. "The light was out, and I convinced myself that it was a raccoon knocking over the garbage can. I should have checked."

Again, Link squeezed her fingers. "No you shouldn't have. You shouldn't have even stayed up there once you heard something. I'm the one who's at fault." He looked at Bronson. "She told me she'd heard something, but I didn't take her seriously. I figured she'd been reading so many of those mysteries she likes that she was just imagining things."

"Do you remember what night this happened?" Bronson had his pencil poised above his notebook.

Annie thought back, then nodded, remembering. "It happened four nights ago."

"Good. That's more than we had. But if you hear any more strange noises, you call. Okay?"

The detective asked more questions, jotting down their answers. It was an hour before he left. He apologized for not having enough men available to offer Link any special protection, but he warned Link to be careful and to get in touch with him if he received anything suspicious, especially any packages he hadn't ordered or bulky letters. He told Annie to be equally careful. "I'm not sure our man cares who he injures in the process."

"You're sure it's a man?" she asked.

Bronson shook his head. "We're not sure of anything."

Annie returned to the great room after letting Detective Bronson out. Link watched her walk toward the sofa. He knew what he had to do. "I want you out of here," he said firmly. "Pack your bags and get."

"Your doctor wanted me to stay for a day or two more." She moved the chair the detective had sat in back to its original place.

"I don't care what Nelson wanted. You're to leave now."

She nodded, as if agreeing, and went on straightening the furniture. She was acting as if nothing had happened, as if he'd simply had another visitor and now she was tidying up afterward. Finally, she paused and looked at him. "I'm not going."

She had the prettiest blue eyes he'd ever seen, and the sexiest mouth, but she obviously didn't have a brain in her head. "I'm giving you no choice. You're out of here. Done. Finished. Fired."

He was going to miss her. He would miss those smiles of hers, and her laughter. Even her demands and arguments. He would miss the scent of her perfume, and the way her jeans hugged her legs, and how her small breasts pressed against those colorful tops she always wore. He would even miss that crazy nightshirt with its fish design.

She walked over to stand in front of him, put her hands on her hips, and shook her head. "Nope. I'm not leaving. Not until those twenty-four hours are up, and maybe not even then."

Stunned, he stared at her. "What do you mean you're not leaving?"

NINE

I needed to disappear and do it fast. I didn't want to leave the houseboat, but someone was trying to kill me, and I didn't like the idea of being a sitting duck. There was one place I could go. Question was, would she welcome me?

—Danger Zone

"I mean just exactly what I said." Annie wasn't about to back down on this. "I'm not leaving. At least not until you do. Don't you understand? You're the one who has to get out of this house. Link, someone is trying to kill you."

"All right then, I'll go somewhere."

"Where? Where will you go?"

"I don't know."

He glared at her, and she knew she was pushing, but he needed to be pushed. Their harrowing ride down the hill that morning had scared her. Sure, she'd suggested a bomb as the cause for the explosion in his lab, but until Detective Bronson confirmed it, the idea had only been a suggestion. Now it was a reality, just as those cut brakes were a reality.

"I could go to my uncle's," Link said with a shrug. "He's out of town."

"You could," she agreed. "Or you could come to my place."

Link stared at her, and she knew he thought she was crazy. Well, maybe she was. Why invite the wolf into your house? Why ask for trouble?

She didn't have an answer.

"Look," she said. "I know you don't need a live-in nurse, but you haven't recuperated one hundred percent, and your doctor did want me to keep an eye on you for a couple of days. After that, well, you'll just be there. Think of it this way. This person who's trying to kill you may know where your uncle lives, may know he's out of town, and may figure that's exactly where you'd go. On the other hand, I don't think anyone you know would know where I live. And who's going to think you'd go with me? After all, everyone knows you don't like women."

He snorted and let his eyes scan her body. "If I don't like women, why do you turn me on?"

His look sent her pulse racing, and she remembered the night he'd kissed her. No, Link didn't dislike women, at least not physically. Still, she knew she was right.

"Okay, let me rephrase that. I don't think many people would expect you to move in with a woman. You're not exactly generous with your praise of the female species. Some of the things you've said to me—" She stopped, disturbed by what she was thinking. "Could you have made some woman angry enough to want to kill you?"

"Well, considering the only two women I've had much contact with in the last year have been you and Diane, and since I don't think Diane's plotting my murder, that leaves you." He lifted his eyebrows. "Have I irritated you enough that you would want to kill me?"

"Torture, maybe. Kill, no. And I certainly wouldn't do it with me in the car with you." The reminder turned her somber. "I'm serious about this, Link. I know you don't think much of those mysteries I'm always reading, but one thing you'll find in those books is when the hero is in danger, he goes into hiding, he doesn't sit around and wait for someone to take another potshot at him."

"And of course this hero always goes running to a beautiful woman who risks her life and gives him shelter."

"Of course."

"And how many of these women end up getting killed in the story?"

She wouldn't consider that. "Link, nothing is going to happen to me. First of all, if you do this, you tell no one where you're going. Or, at least, you only tell the people you really trust. And while you're at my place, you stay out of sight. You wouldn't need to go anywhere. You could use my garage to work on that fuel cell of yours. That way no one would see you going to and from my place. No one would know you were there. There would be no danger."

"You're seriously offering your place as a lab and a shelter?"

He frowned, but she could tell he was considering the

idea, so she decided she'd better add a few disclaimers. "You wouldn't be living as fancy as this. My place isn't anything to write home about. It's a two-bedroom tract home, and those bedrooms are postage-stamp size."

His smile came immediately. "Are you inviting me to your bed, Annie?"

"No." That would truly be risky. "I'm inviting you to my house, nothing more."

"You said no making love with a patient. If I go with you, it wouldn't be as your patient. Are you going to deny there's an attraction between us?"

She wanted to. "It doesn't matter what there is," she said firmly. "What I'm offering is a working relationship, a safe place for you to stay, and nothing more."

"And do you always invite men you barely know to move in with you?"

"I think I know you a little more than 'barely' and this is a unique situation."

"Yes, someone is trying to murder me. What you should be doing is getting far, far away from me."

She should, she knew, but not because someone was trying to kill him. Bringing him to her house was a crazy idea. She couldn't deny that she was attracted to him. The physical desire was there—raging at times—yet he was exactly the type of man she didn't want to get involved with.

"Look, it's up to you," she said, trying to keep her feelings out of the matter. "Go to your uncle's if you want. Fire me, if you want. But I think I'm offering a better solution." Then she remembered one thing. "That is, unless you're allergic to cats."

He said nothing, simply looked at her, and she knew he was weighing the pros and cons. Finally, he smiled. "I can't get rid of you, can I?"

"Ever read Stephen King's *Misery*?" Link shook his head, and she went on. "In the book, a guy who's a writer has an accident and ends up in the care of a nurse who happens to be a fan of his, only she doesn't like what he's doing to one of his characters. The poor writer becomes her prisoner."

"Oh, now there's an encouraging thought. I go from someone trying to kill me to imprisonment." He pushed himself up from the sofa and balanced on his crutches. Once stable, he faced her. "The answer is no, I'm not allergic to cats."

"So you'll come?"

As she waited for his response, a giddy sensation churning in her stomach, a tiny voice in her head warned her that she was making a mistake. She knew she was, that he was right, she was attracted to him and she wasn't handling this in a professional manner. Nevertheless, she couldn't stop herself.

"Yes, I'll come," he finally said.

Before they left his place, Link called his uncle. Actually, since his uncle should be somewhere between London and Paris, Link called the hotel in Paris where his uncle was scheduled to be staying that night. He kept the message brief. The desk clerk on the other end of the line spoke broken English, and Link wasn't sure how much she truly understood.

He grumbled when he had to ride in Annie's Geo. He could tell from her smirk that she thought it was funny. Here his car, his beautiful Jaguar that cost close to eighty thousand dollars, was in a body shop and he was forced to ride in a car that probably cost less than what his repair bill was going to be.

Detective Bronson had assured them that one of his men had checked out Annie's car thoroughly. Still she tested the brakes several times before picking up any speed going down the hill. As they drove past the house where they'd managed to pull the Jaguar off the road, Annie slowed so they could look. They'd definitely done a job on the mailbox, and tire tracks marred the lawn, the marks clearly showing the sideways skid of the Jag before it crashed into the eucalyptus tree. Link was sure he'd get a bill for those damages too.

"Could have been worse," Annie said.

She was right, he knew. Material things could be replaced or fixed. A life was more valuable. The loss of his father and brother had driven that message home. He hated to admit how much he missed them still. It seemed as if everyone he cared for left him, one way or another.

"I shouldn't have let you talk me into this," he said as Annie turned onto the road toward the Caldecott tunnel. "This is ridiculous. I'm putting you in danger."

She laughed and faked a gravelly voice. "Danger is my business."

He didn't see the humor. "I'm serious, Annie. Take me back to my place. This isn't a game. You could get hurt. You could have been hurt this morning."

Her expression turned equally serious. "Maybe I

could have been, but I wasn't. Stop worrying. Unless someone's following us right now"—she glanced into her rearview mirror—"and I don't see anyone, who's going to know where you are? And even if someone suspects you might go with me, I have an unlisted number. They're not going to be able to look up my name and find my address."

"And what will your family think when they find out you have a man living with you?"

She laughed sarcastically. "I don't see my family all that much, and I don't care what they think." She glanced his way. "Actually, if they do find out I have a man living with me, they'll think there's hope after all. My father and brother still can't understand why I divorced Dennis. They thought I was making a big deal over nothing. A woman should understand a man's nature, right? A 'real' man needs more than one woman. Right?"

"It still hurts, doesn't it?"

She merely shrugged.

That she'd been hurt by a man made her taking him to her house all the more mystifying. Maybe her father and brother thought a woman should understand a man's nature, but Link knew he would never understand a woman's nature. If ever a woman should leave him, it was now. But not Annie. No, here she was, driving him to her house. Protecting him. Risking her own life.

It was crazy.

Angling the back of the seat down so he could stretch out more, Link closed his eyes and tried to think of anyone he'd angered or upset in the past year. He found his thoughts drifting to the sound of the car's engine. It was

definitely not the purr of a Jaguar engine—or the roar—
but it was steady. The rhythm was absolutely mesmeriz-
ing.

Annie woke Link when they reached her house. He
got out of her car awkwardly, and she had a feeling his
body was as sore as hers was becoming. The air bags
might have saved their lives, or at least saved them from
serious injuries, but those things weren't gentle when
they hit your chest. Considering Link's body hadn't completely healed from the beating it had taken from the
explosion in his lab, she knew he'd be hurting for several
days to come.

He stood on his crutches, staring at her place. She
gave him a moment to take it all in, from the curling
wooden shingles on the roof; to the off-white stucco exte-
rior, replete with stains and cracks; to the tiny overgrown
lawn in front. Brown spots dotted the grass, where the
neighbors' dogs had left their calling cards, and weeds
grew through cracks in the walk leading to the front door.
The one-car garage was on the right, as they faced the
house. She'd parked in the drive rather than pulling all
the way in. It gave Link more room to maneuver.

"Not exactly a palace," she finally said. "But I can
afford the payments."

He looked down at her. "It's nice, really it is."

"Liar," she said, smiling, and opened the hatchback of
the Geo. Considering the small size of the car, they had
packed in quite a bit. Enough for a two-week stay on

Link's part. She hoped the police would have something by then.

"Follow me," she said, lugging two of the suitcases and heading up the walk toward her front door.

Inside, she set the suitcases down and immediately began opening windows to air out the place. First she showed Link the garage, where he could work. The laundry room joined the garage to the kitchen and eating area. In the living room, she gave him instructions on how to turn on the television, though she'd noticed he rarely watched TV. In that way he was different from her ex, who was always either eating, sleeping, or watching TV. That or having sex, with her and with others.

Next came the bathroom and the two bedrooms. She merely pointed into her bedroom as she passed it. Link stopped at the doorway and looked in. When he stepped inside her room, she came back.

He was exploring the small bedroom, keeping his crutches close to his body as he squeezed through the narrow passage between the end of her bed and her dresser. For a moment he paused to glance over the pictures she had out: the family portrait taken when she and her brother and sister were still in school, the snapshots of her mother, of her sister and her husband, and the one taken the previous summer of her dad and brother with a string of fish.

Link glanced her way. "That's the family," she answered, and stepped into the room, walking over so she could identify each member.

"Your sister doesn't have the spark you do," he said when Annie pointed her out.

"Alice is more—" She wasn't sure how to explain her sister's personality. "Compliant."

"Compliant?" Link repeated, his gaze on her.

Annie shrugged. She might as well tell him. "She's like my mother. A doormat. They're the kind of woman every man wants: obedient and ready to jump at every command. In their eyes, it's a man's world and they are merely here to serve."

"How did you end up the way you are?"

She knew what he meant. "Ornery?"

"Full of sass. Feisty. I would certainly never use the word 'compliant' to describe you."

She grinned. "Let's see. Dennis said I was stubborn, short-tempered, and irrational." She shook her head. "I was such a fool to marry him, and don't ask me why I did. I blame it on a foolish belief that I could change him. Trust me, you don't change people. You either accept them the way they are, or you don't marry them."

"Or you leave them." He said it with no emotion, and Annie wished she'd kept her mouth shut.

"I guess you're right. Actually, in your case, your ex-wife couldn't accept that you did change from the man she thought she'd married. With Dennis and me, we simply never should have married. I wanted someone who was faithful, who treated me as an equal. He wanted someone like my mother or sister."

"Too bad for him," Link said, facing her. He leaned on his crutches so he could reach out and touch the side of her face. "He didn't know what he had."

The brush of his fingertips over her cheek was no more than a whisper of a touch, its gentleness stirring her heart. She looked up at his face and knew she'd made a big mistake, she never should have brought him to her house. She should have taken his advice and run when she could, for now she knew she was lost. Whether they were right for each other or not no longer mattered. She cared for him, cared more than a nurse for a patient. Cared more than one friend for another. With that one simple touch, he'd stolen her heart.

"Link?" she said cautiously, afraid he might kiss her. "I—I think . . ." She wasn't sure what she thought, but she knew she had to get out of that room, away from the lure of her bed and Link's captivating gaze.

"I think—" She swallowed hard and stepped back. "I'd better go next door and get my cat."

Link finished the tour of Annie's house on his own. She'd been right. It was small and certainly not what he was used to. At least, not used to now. He hadn't always lived in luxury. After his divorce, his finances had forced him to live in an apartment that was co-inhabited by cockroaches and rats. During that period of his life, he could have turned to his father for help, but he'd been too proud. And he was glad he had made it on his own, even though his uncle had periodically begged him to come back to the family company and work on tool designs. Believing in himself had paid off. Most inventors couldn't say as much, but he'd been lucky. He'd chased the right dream, come up with the right idea at the right time.

He was back in her living room when Annie returned. In her arms she carried a Siamese cat, a bag of cat litter, and a litter box. The cat wiggled out of her arms the moment she stepped into the house, landing on the carpeting on all four feet. He twitched his tail and strolled off to the kitchen with a plaintive yowl.

"And that's Ziggy," Annie said, watching her cat walk away.

"He has your eyes," Link said.

"He also has an attitude."

"Must be hereditary."

She wrinkled her nose at him and carried the litter box and bag of cat litter to the laundry room. "Is it going to be big enough?" she called back to him.

"You mean the house?" He followed her through the kitchen, stopping at the doorway to the laundry room. Annie was leaning over, dumping the cat litter into the box, and the cat was beside her, watching.

"No, the garage," she said, straightening. The cat immediately stepped into the litter box, checking it out, and Annie opened the door to the garage. "I'll clean it up." She pointed toward several boxes and tools scattered around the space. "Straighten things up and sweep it all out. My car doesn't need to be in here, so you can use all of the space. You'll just have to tell me what you'll need."

"Dan can get what I need." He'd decided that already.

Annie closed the door and turned toward him. "You trust him? You're sure he's not the one trying to kill you?"

"Dan?" Link laughed at the idea. "No, he's not the one. I'd trust Dan with my life."

"You are," she said seriously.

Link realized she was right. He was trusting Dan and he was trusting her. But who else could he trust?

"I wouldn't tell Diane," Annie said.

That surprised him. "Why not?"

She shook her head. "I'm not sure why. Maybe because there are so many coincidences between that trip she took and the timing of that bomb."

"She was on the cruise the night you heard the noise near my car."

"But we're not sure that's when the brakes were tampered with."

He considered her answer, then nodded. "Okay, we don't tell Diane. What about Jeff Yamaguchi?"

"It's your decision, but the fewer people who know, the better."

Link considered his relationship with Jeff. The younger man had been a good assistant, and Link didn't think he harbored any resentment, but Jeff was now working in a field not dissimilar to Link's. Eliminating the competition might be one way to ensure yourself a job in the future. Not that he wanted to believe Jeff would do that.

"We won't tell Jeff," he said, hating the idea of analyzing each of his friends for possible motives.

"Your uncle?"

"He'll need to know."

"Anyone else?"

Link thought about that. "I guess it doesn't say much about me, but I can't think of anyone else. For the last six months, I've been living the life of a recluse, devoting my energy to that fuel cell. I have no social life, belong to no committees or organizations. Except for my uncle, I have no family." He grimaced. "It's pretty sad. I could disappear tomorrow, and no one would care."

Annie touched his hand where it rested on his crutch. "You've disappeared today, and I care."

Ron Sheffield tipped the man who'd carried his bags from the taxi to the front desk, then glanced at his watch. Although it was nearly midnight in Paris, it would be the middle of the afternoon in California. Once he was up in his room, he would call Link. Link was to have gone to the doctor's that day. The way he sounded every time Ron called, Link was doing great.

Maybe too great.

Why his nephew insisted on persisting with this fuel cell design was beyond Ron. Another year, things would be different. Another year, and it wouldn't matter.

Why couldn't he simply take a break and let his body heal? Not Link, though. No, he had to do everything right now. Buy that big house on the hill. Buy that Jaguar. Link loved the fact that he'd made it after being so down on his luck. Made it without any of their help, without giving up his ideals, and without coming to work for the family business.

His pride would do him in. Ron wondered how many times he'd told Link that. Hundreds of times, he was sure.

Link should have come to work for Sheffield's Tools. If he could invent all those gadgets for automobiles, he could have invented a few new tools. But no, not Link. He had to go his own way.

Ron knew he was tired. This trip was taking a lot out of him, flying across the country and then across the Atlantic, staying in one hotel after another. Late-night arrivals and early-morning meetings could wear a man out. And now, for the first time this trip, he was in a country where English wasn't the native language. That is, if you considered what they spoke in England to be English. Gads, half the time he didn't understand what those people were saying.

"*Bonsoir*, monsieur," the desk clerk greeted him. "You have a reservation?"

"Sheffield," Ron said, pulling out his wallet. "Four nights."

"Ah, Monsieur Sheffield, I have a message for you." The clerk turned and pulled a note from one of the boxes behind him.

He handed Ron the note. Ron read it once, then again. Not that there was much to read:

Something happened today. Have decided to stay somewhere else. I'll call tomorrow. Link.

"That's all he said?" Ron asked the clerk.

"I am sorry, monsieur. I did not take the message. It was one of the other clerks, and she is now off. Is there a problem?"

"No, no problem," Ron said, rereading the note and frowning. Then he looked back at the clerk. "I need to get up to my room. I need to make a call."

TEN

The hardest part of any murder investigation is informing the victim's family. Why I'd volunteered in this case, I didn't know. Perhaps because I had so many unanswered questions, and I hoped the dead man's widow could supply a few answers.
— Dead Men Don't Answer

Annie wondered if she should let her mother know she was home, then decided against it. Her family didn't expect her back until the end of the week. It was better to leave it at that. The fewer who knew what was going on, the safer Link would be.

Of course, she'd told her neighbor. Mrs. Moore would have called the police if she'd seen lights on in the house last night. And Annie had no intention of leaving her cat over there. She'd missed him.

She watched Ziggy finish the food she'd put down for him. He licked the dish clean, then strolled out of the kitchen and into the living room. He'd slept with her the night before, but this morning he was acting totally indifferent. "Just like a man," she muttered to herself.

The ring of the telephone startled her, and she grabbed for it. Link, as far as she knew, was still asleep, and she didn't want to wake him. After all he'd been through, he needed his rest.

She answered cautiously, unsure who would be calling. Other than Detective Bronson and Dan Zura, no one was supposed to know Link and she were in Lafayette. As Annie listened to the voice on the other end of the line, she realized that was no longer true. The Glencove Home Care Agency knew she was home.

She heard a door open down the hallway. Looking in that direction, she saw a pair of crutches come out of her second bedroom, then Link. His hair was mussed and he was wearing only shorts, no shirt. He looked her way, then headed for the bathroom.

Annie watched the supple play of his back muscles as he maneuvered the crutches. He wasn't all sinew and brawn, not like Dennis or her brother or most of the jocks she knew. Link's body had a lean, wiry look, the look of a man who used his brain, not his body. Yet she knew from the hours she'd worked to keep his muscles supple that he was no ninety-pound weakling. She remembered, too, how his body had felt pressed against hers the night he'd kissed her.

As she watched him disappear into the bathroom, she smiled. His strength was truly deceptive. He'd caught her off guard that night. Surprised, she'd succumbed to his kisses and to her own emotions. She would have to make sure that didn't happen again. For her sanity, she needed to keep up her guard.

A pause on the other end of the line brought Annie back to her telephone call. "I can understand your concern, Kathy," she said into the phone.

The voice on the other end belonged to Kathy Ball, the Glencove Home Care Agency secretary. Considering what Kathy had just said, Annie understood why she was getting a call and how the agency knew where she was. Although she didn't like lying, she knew it was necessary. "I just can't help you, Kathy . . . or his uncle. I don't know where Dr. Sheffield is."

Annie knew she'd be asked what had happened, and during the night she'd thought of how she'd answer. Once Kathy gave her a chance to speak, Annie began her story. "There was an accident yesterday. It happened while I was driving Sheffield to his doctor's appointment. He had me drive his car, a very expensive Jaguar, and a dog ran out in the road in front of me. I guess I hit the brakes too hard because we went into a spin and hit a tree."

Kathy interrupted, and Annie let her, distracted as she was as Link came out of the bathroom. His hair had been tamed some, but he still looked frazzled, and his jaw was covered with a day's growth of beard. He headed down the hallway toward her, and she felt a strange tightening of her stomach muscles.

It had been a long time since she'd entertained a half-dressed man in her house, and though she'd spent eleven days with Link, having him here made a difference in their relationship. She watched him draw near and raised a finger to her lips, signaling for him not to speak.

"I'm . . . I'm all right," she said to Kathy, the slight tremble in her voice not faked. Around Link, she was never all right. "Shaken," she added. "I feel like I was hit by a cement truck."

Link nodded his agreement, and she pointed toward the coffeepot on the counter, the carafe half-full of fresh coffee, then toward the cupboard that held her supply of mugs.

"A doctor checked us both out. Nothing damaged, other than the car. I guess I don't need to tell you I was fired."

Link nodded his agreement to that, too, and she scowled at him.

"Yeah, can you imagine that?" she said into the phone. "He fired me. Just because I put a few dents in his car."

Link swiped his hand through the air to indicate she'd wiped out the whole side of his car. He didn't need to tell her. She'd seen the Jaguar.

"No, I don't know where he's gone. After he fired me, I got my stuff and left. I do know where I'd like to tell him to go." She smiled superficially at Link, and he gave her a matching phony smile.

"You say his uncle is looking for him? Called you this morning?" Annie held up two fingers when Kathy said how many times Ron had called the home care agency. "He wanted my number?"

Annie wondered if Kathy had given it to Link's uncle.

In a moment, she knew. "Good," she said. "He doesn't need to know my number. I couldn't help him, and I don't need another Sheffield lecturing me on my responsibilities as a nurse. If his nephew wants him to know where he is, I'm sure he'll tell him."

She hoped that would end the matter. Kathy reminded her of a flaw in her story. "Another job?" Annie watched Link maneuver with his crutches to get to the table, holding on to a mug of coffee. "No, don't tell Lois I'm available for another assignment. Not yet. I'm—I'm going to take a few days off to recuperate. Hitting that tree really shook me up. Why don't we say, 'Don't call me, I'll call you.'" She laughed, then wished she hadn't. Her ribs did hurt.

After saying good-bye, she hung up the phone and looked at Link. "Your uncle is trying to get hold of you. He called the agency for my number. Did you tell him you were going to be here?"

"No, just that I'd call him. Which I suppose I'd better do." Link glanced at the clock on the wall. "First I'll have my coffee, then I'll get the number of the hotel he's at." He shook his head, smiling slightly. "He worries about me too much. Fusses."

"He cares about you."

"I guess." Link sipped his coffee, then sighed in satisfaction and leaned back in his chair. "I think, though, that I'm not going to tell him where I'm at. I liked what you told that caller. It's better if everyone thinks I fired you." Again he smiled. "Sounds like what I would do. And that way, if Uncle Ron happens to slip and mention what's going on to anyone, he's not going to pass on any information that might involve you."

It made sense to Annie. She nodded her agreement.

Living with Annie, Link discovered, was a mixture of pleasure and torture. The next five days went by quickly, his time devoted to setting up an area where he could work on rebuilding the prototype of his fuel cell. Dan brought him the equipment and materials he needed, and Link began putting plates, frames, and catalysts together. Maneuvering around on crutches slowed him down, and a sudden heat wave wasn't helping. It was barely two in the afternoon when he gave up working in the suffocating heat of the closed garage. Heading back into the house, he stopped in the laundry room to watch Annie. She was in the kitchen, standing in front of the refrigerator with the freezer door open, her head almost in the unit.

The halter top and shorts she wore might be keeping her cool, but the skimpy outfit didn't help lower his internal thermostat. When she glanced his way, her sweat-dampened bangs sticking to her forehead and her smile innocently sexy, he knew there was no way he could live with her without making love with her. His doctorate might be in physics, but he knew enough about chemistry to recognize a volatile situation.

With the sweep of her hand, Annie pushed her dampened hair back from her face, the gesture tightening her halter top and pressing the fabric against her breasts, giving him a teasing suggestion of what the material covered.

"It's so hot," she said. "I thought I'd make some lemonade."

"Looks more like you're using the freezer as an air conditioner." Which wasn't a bad idea, he decided. He needed something to cool his thoughts.

"I guess I was." She pulled out the can of frozen juice and closed the freezer door, then looked at him. "You must be cooking out there. I just heard on the radio that the temperature is ninety-eight degrees. Can you believe that? Ninety-eight degrees in April?"

He believed it. "I think it's a hundred and forty in the garage." He tapped his fingertips against his cast, then swung himself into the kitchen on his crutches. "I'm ready to cut this damned thing off."

She glanced down at the cast on his right leg, then back at his face. "Does it itch?"

"Terribly."

"I remember breaking my arm one summer when I was a kid." She grimaced. "The itching nearly drove me crazy. Sit down." she pointed toward a chair at the kitchen table. "Let's get you cooled off."

With her in that outfit, he considered that an impossible task, but he sat in the chair she offered, glad to be off his left leg. Even his armpits were raw from the crutches.

Annie moved the fan on the floor so it was directed toward him, then she started the lemonade. "I've got to get my air conditioner fixed. It broke down last fall, but I thought I'd have a while before I needed it this year."

"I'll work on it for you," he said. Considering how much she was doing for him—moving him into her house and turning over her garage—it was the least he could do.

She set a glass of iced lemonade in front of him, then surprised him by running her fingers through his hair. If she was trying to cool him off, that wasn't the way. Cocking an eyebrow, he looked up at her.

She grinned. "You need a haircut, mister."

She walked away from him, and Link had a feeling he knew what was coming. For days, she'd been nagging him about his hair. "You're fussing again," he called after her, but she didn't answer, just kept walking.

He ran his own fingers through his hair, lifting it from his neck. She was right. He did need a haircut.

She had a pair of scissors, a comb, a spray bottle of water, and a bath towel in her hands when she walked back into the kitchen. "You don't have to do this," he said, knowing she expected an argument from him.

"I don't have to do anything," she reminded him. "Now, stop your grumbling. This will make you cooler."

He grinned. She really was a sassy thing. Funny part was, he was getting to like it.

She placed everything but the towel on the table. That she draped over his shoulders, then pulled it away. "Take off your shirt."

"You are getting downright bossy," he said, but did as she'd ordered, pulling his T-shirt over his head and tossing it onto a nearby chair.

Again, she placed the towel over his shoulders, bringing it around his neck. She picked up the spray bottle and began squirting water on his hair. "You say bossy, but you know what's wrong with me?" She didn't give him a chance to answer. "I'm bored." She ran her fingers through his hair, lifting it from his scalp. "I think it's time for me to go back to work, Link. I'm not good at just sitting around doing nothing."

The tingle that ran down his spine at her touch gave him all sorts of ideas of what she could do . . . what they could do together to keep her from getting bored.

When she stepped to his side, Link sucked in a breath and looked straight ahead, not at the cotton halter that was at eye level. Although he wouldn't describe her as busty, the creamy flesh her top exposed was very enticing. "You have me to take care of," he said, aware that his voice was husky.

"You don't need any care," she said, moving around to his other side and spraying his hair. "Don't forget, if things had been different, I would have been out of a job two or three days ago."

"If things had been different, you wouldn't have had this job in the first place." He tried to ignore the soft brush of her knuckles against his neck, but ignoring Annie when she was this close was all but impossible. There was her perfume, her voice—

She set the spray bottle down and picked up the scissors and comb. "The home care agency called again this morning. They wanted to know if I was ready for another assignment."

He moved his head to look up at her. "What did you tell them?"

"I told them yes." She placed her hands on the sides of his head, straightening his position again. "It's time for me to earn a paycheck again."

Once more, he twisted his head to look at her. "What about the money I'm paying you?"

"What money?" She grinned. "My job with you ended several days ago. Even if you add on the two days your doctor asked me to stay on, that leaves me unemployed for three days. And since we said you fired me—that was our story, remember?—I think the agency might find it a bit suspicious if you paid my salary for those two days. Lois is probably waiting for you to call and threaten to sue the agency because I wrecked your car."

He snorted. "I'm not suing anyone, and we don't have to go through the agency. This is between you and me."

"But what are you going to pay me for? All you're getting is a bed to sleep in, three meals, and no air-conditioning. That's not exactly worth what I make as a nurse."

"I'm also getting a garage to work in, access to a phone, taxi service if and when I need it, and—" He realized she'd straightened his head again and was snipping away at his hair. "Barber service," he finished. "It's worth it to me to pay your wages, and if you want more to do, I need an assistant." He'd realized that earlier that day. "Dan can get the materials I need, but he can't stick around and help, he has his own job. And since we're not letting Diane or Jeff know where I am, that leaves me without an assistant. What do you say? Interested?"

He didn't move his head, but smiled at the idea he'd just proposed. A little more than two weeks ago, he hadn't wanted her anywhere near him. Now he was asking her to be his assistant. The explosion and his car running into that tree had to have affected his brain. How was he going to get anything done on that fuel cell with Annie nearby? Having her standing behind him cutting his hair was bad enough. Anytime she was around, he was tempted to touch her.

"You want me to be your assistant?" She continued clipping, his hair falling onto the towel and floor. "And what do I tell my boss? She's going to think it's strange if I don't take a job. She knows I need the money."

"Tell her—" He thought up a quick excuse. "Call her tomorrow morning and tell her you got an emergency call during the night. Your aunt in Peoria is ill and you've got to fly back there to be with her. Tell her that you'll probably be out of town for a couple weeks."

"I don't have an aunt in Peoria."

"Does your boss or anyone at the agency know that?"

"No." She chuckled. "It might work. So, what does an assistant to Dr. Link Sheffield do?"

"Keeps me happy."

"Oh, yeah?" The lift of her eyebrows suggested her suspicions.

Link knew she was right to be suspicious. What he had in mind for her was different from what he required from most of his assistants. Nevertheless, he smiled innocently. "My assistant takes notes, fetches things when I need them, and holds parts in place."

"In other words, a gofer."

"That about sums it up. It's being near me, watching a genius at work, that makes it all worth it."

"Gads, you're full of yourself, aren't you?"

He shrugged. "What can I say? That's what I've been told. They want to work for me because they want to see how I work. How my mind works," he said more precisely.

"And how does your mind work?" She set down the scissors and turned him in his chair so he was facing her, then stood back to look at her handiwork.

"I don't think you want to know," he said, his gaze traveling down the front of her.

"Hmm." She frowned and leaned forward to brush a lock of hair behind his ear.

He wasn't sure if she didn't understand what he meant, or if she didn't want to understand. He knew, with her this close, he couldn't resist the temptation. Reaching forward, he snagged her by the waist and pulled her to him.

"Link!" she squealed, but automatically moved her feet so she wouldn't run into his cast. That put her into position so he could pull her down onto his lap. Before she could react, he had her seated facing him, her shorts-clad bottom resting on his thighs and her face level with his.

"Dr. Sheffield!" she said, wiggling to get away.

He noticed she always used his formal title when he moved their relationship beyond the nurse/patient realm. He supposed she thought it would create a gap between them. It didn't. Keeping a secure hold around her waist, he brought her closer to his hips and knew exactly when she felt his erection. Her sudden stillness and the widening of her eyes told him. If she'd had any question of what was on his mind, she had her answer.

This time when she said his name, she dropped the doctor business and there was a breathless quality to her voice. He could see, from the rise and fall of her chest, that her breathing wasn't normal. "What?" he asked, leaning forward to brush a kiss over her cheek.

He tasted the salty sweat that covered her body and knew he was as sweaty. The towel she'd placed over his shoulders had fallen to the floor, and he was naked from the waist up. The halter top she had on could hardly be called a covering. Flesh touched flesh.

"This isn't a good idea," she said, but didn't move.

"I think it's a very good idea," he murmured, and teased her with a kiss on her other cheek.

"We shouldn't—"

She didn't finish. Perhaps because he'd silenced her words by touching his lips to hers. Or perhaps because he'd untied the cloth strings around her neck. Her halter fell loose, dropping to her waist, and he knew her breasts were bared.

He kissed Annie with a longing he hadn't known for years. Kissed her and tasted her, and then with one hand, touched her, sliding his palm over a hardened nipple.

He heard her groan, or maybe it was him. She felt so good, so soft and yet firm, warm and pliant. She felt exactly as he'd imagined she would feel.

He knew she'd stopped resisting when she slid her hands around his neck, kneading his shoulders with her fingers. Now she kissed him back, silently making promises and giving in to a passion that neither could control.

He untied the halter string around her ribs and back and removed the bit of cloth, dropping it to the floor. Then he held her close, pressing her breasts against his chest. The sensations spiraling through him increased the pressure in his loins, and he knew he wanted the rest of their clothing off, wanted to be inside of her, surrounded by her. With the thrust of his tongue, he communicated his desires, and from the catch in her breath, he knew she understood.

He eased her back, bringing their hips into closer contact, and she looked at him with smoky blue eyes that said more than words. She watched as he leaned forward and sucked a nipple into his mouth, and she groaned and ran her fingers through his hair, holding him to her.

The fan blew air across their bodies, but the heat building within them couldn't be cooled. He wasn't sure how they were going to accomplish this, but he wanted her, and he wanted her now. Slipping one hand down to the waist of her shorts, he began pushing them lower.

Whether it was his chair creaking as he shifted his position or simply her internal warning system finally clicking in, Annie realized the foolishness of what they were doing. Pulling back, she caught Link off guard and twisted out of his hold. Quickly she slid off his lap, took a step to the side, and was out of reach. Her entire body shaking and her breathing erratic, she leaned against the kitchen counter, the Formica cool against her heated skin.

"Annie?" It was all he said, just her name, but his eyes, dark and heavy with desire, said so much more. He wanted her.

By his feet lay her halter top, and she knew she should cover herself, but she didn't bother. Modesty seemed ridiculous at this point. Cloth certainly wasn't concealing his desire for her, his erection a hard outline against his shorts.

She'd felt that hardness pressing against the juncture of her thighs and had known the desire to have him inside her. She still felt the ache, and knew he could assuage it. It took all of her willpower to stand where she was.

"This has got to stop," she said, sounding nowhere near as firm as she wanted.

"Why?" he asked. His gaze never left her face.

"Because." She couldn't think of an excuse to give without revealing her vulnerability.

His eyebrows lifted. "Because you're afraid?"

"Because it's wrong." Wrong for her at least.

"How can it be wrong?" He pushed himself up to a standing position. "We are two grown adults. We're attracted to each other." He reached over to where he'd leaned his crutches against the table. "I've got some condoms with me. In the bedroom. If I use them, who is it going to hurt?"

She knew who it would hurt. She would be hurt. Link could make love with her, relieve his need, and that would be it. Oh, sure, maybe they'd do it more than once during his stay, but it wouldn't mean anything to him. Certainly not the same as it would to her. Dennis had explained how it was. A man didn't need to be emotionally involved, he'd said. It was the nature of men to chase after women.

Well maybe it was, but it wasn't her nature. She didn't make love simply to relieve a desire. When she made love, there had to be an emotional commitment—on both sides.

"Annie?" Link said, coming closer.

"No." She backed away, shaking her head.

"Whoa." He stopped where he was. "Don't run off."

She watched him warily, but stood still. "Then forget this. I can't have you staying here if I'm going to be constantly afraid you're going to jump my bones."

"There's a chemistry between us."

"So? Ignore it."

"Can you?"

"Yes," she lied.

For a moment, he said nothing, then he muttered something and swung past her on his crutches. She watched him go and felt tears stinging her eyes. For him, it was chemistry. For her, it was so much more. And what hurt the most was that stopping him wasn't really going to help. Although she'd kept him from making love with her, she hadn't been able to stop herself from falling in love with him. Over and over, she'd told herself Link was wrong for her, yet still he'd slipped through her barriers. All she could hope was that by not making love with him, she would minimize the pain when he left.

ELEVEN

I've always worked alone, but you know, sometimes a partner helps. I sure didn't like looking down the barrel of that forty-five, not when Jake Fortrell had a crazed look in his eyes. I didn't know what I was going to do, and then Myrna screamed.
— It Takes Two to Tango

Annie discovered working with Link was not easy. He was a perfectionist and a taskmaster. Maybe she wasn't doing any nursing, but she didn't have time to get bored. Which was good. Link's stay of two weeks turned into four, then more. As far as Lois Greenman was concerned, Annie's aunt in Peoria wasn't doing well at all. As for Annie's family, a few calls now and then let them know she was all right and they thought she was still working in Oakland, that the job had been extended. The only ones who knew where she and Link were and what was going on were Detective Bronson, who kept them updated on what the police had learned, which was little; Link's doctor, who changed Link's cast to a walking cast the third week; and Dan Zura, who came by often to bring supplies, help, or simply visit.

Annie liked Dan, and she suspected he knew how she felt about Link. Link was the one who was oblivious to her feelings. He'd taken her at her word—no sex—and their relationship had settled into a routine, albeit an unusual one. He bossed her around when she was helping him with the fuel cell. She bossed him around when it came to his eating habits and the exercise she deemed necessary for his continued improvement. And when they weren't bossing each other, they had conversations that fringed on being normal, including some griping about life and the opposite sex.

The afternoon Annie drove him to the doctor's to get his cast removed, she told him about a mystery she'd been reading. "What gripes me," she said, "is they were working as a team, sort of like Nick and Nora."

"Nick and Nora?" Link repeated, watching her as she drove.

"*The Thin Man.*" She glanced his way. "Myrna Loy and William Powell. Dashiell Hammett . . ."

She trailed off, shaking her head, and Link had a feeling she knew he didn't have the foggiest idea what she was talking about. Her attention turned back to her driving, and she went on. "Anyway, in this book I was reading last night, the bad guy has a gun pointed at the hero, and the hero's girlfriend comes in, sees he's in trouble, and drops to the floor, writhing and carrying on as if she's having a seizure. The gunman is distracted and our hero disarms him. But does the girlfriend get any praise? No.

It's the man who gets the glory. Gads, you could tell the book had been written by a man."

Link chuckled. Annie had as many negative attitudes about men as he did about women. "So write your own book. Make the woman the hero and the guy the klutz."

"Well, I have started something." Again she glanced at him. "Mostly, it's just an idea."

"Good." He was pleased. "So what's your book about? Bombs going off? Cars careening down steep curving roads?"

Her smile said she understood his references. "I'm waiting for the resolution of that story before I write it. I can't believe the police have nothing after this long a time. The only positive thing is nothing more has happened."

"Nothing has happened because I'm now your prisoner and no one can get to me."

She shot him a questioning look. "Complaining?"

Link didn't hesitate in answering. "No, not at all. Actually, it's been rather interesting." He didn't add that it had also been very frustrating.

At the doctor's office, Annie discovered that her statement in the car had been wrong. Something more had happened in Link's saga. It was the doctor's receptionist who told her. "A woman called the other day," she said. "She insisted she had to get hold of Dr. Sheffield and wanted a phone number where she could reach him. When I told her I couldn't give out that information, she insisted on talking to Dr. Nelson. I'm sure he didn't tell her anything, but you might want to let Dr. Sheffield know someone's trying to contact him, someone who sounded rather desperate."

"Desperate?" Annie wondered who the woman might be and why she would be desperate to find Link. "Did she give her name?"

"Yes, but I didn't write it down, and for the life of me, I can't remember what it was. I'm really sorry."

"Would it have been Diane?"

The receptionist shrugged. "I just can't remember."

"Well, did she sound young or old?"

"Young," the receptionist said. "I do remember that. Sort of unsure of herself. Maybe nervous?"

Annie relayed the information about the call and caller to Link during the drive back to Lafayette. What she said paralleled the information he'd received. "Nelson remembered who it was. And you're right, it was Diane. He said she sounded very worried, and that she'd heard my life was in danger. He reassured her that I was fine and said he'd have me get in touch with her. What puzzles me is how she would know to call Nelson's office."

"She didn't know he was your doctor?"

Link tried to remember any time he might have mentioned John Nelson's name. "I can't think of why she would. Then again, maybe Dan told her. I know he called her when she got back from her cruise to let her know about the explosion at the lab. Maybe he mentioned it then. I guess I had better call her."

He did once he was back at Annie's. Diane sounded relieved to hear his voice, and Link knew he should have called before. He also understood, immediately, why she'd called his doctor and how she'd known whom to call. "My uncle called you and said my life was in danger?" he repeated.

Diane said she'd been as surprised as he was, but yes, that Ron Sheffield had called her, had said he was worried about Link, and that he hadn't heard from him for a while. He then had asked her to call around and find out what she could. He'd given her a list of names and numbers to call.

"I'm sorry he bothered you," Link said. "I guess I haven't talked to him for quite a while." Link knew it had been far too long and felt a pang of guilt. "I've just been so busy with the fuel cell."

He should have known that comment would prompt Diane to ask why he hadn't called her to help. He gave her the truth. "There was another attempt on my life after your visit, and I'm sort of in hiding."

Diane reacted immediately, questioning him, expressing her concern, and being overly dramatic. Link knew one reason why he liked Annie. Hysterics were not a part of her makeup. She got scared and she got angry, but she didn't cry over things she couldn't control or change. Finally, he stopped Diane's tears. "I'm fine," he said. "Perfectly fine. My cast is off, my cuts are healed, and I'm the same ornery cuss you worked with. The fuel cell is ready to be tested, then packed up and delivered to Detroit. So stop worrying."

Diane's sobs turned to compliments. He was a genius.

He was wonderful. Link rolled his eyes in despair as Annie walked into the kitchen with the groceries she'd picked up at the store. She grinned, set the bags down, and quickly wrote out a note and handed it to him. *Want an excuse to get off?* she'd asked.

He nodded.

Link watched Annie walk out of the kitchen, the little wiggle of her rear end exciting him as always. Diane was still going on about how much she'd appreciated the chance to work with him and how she missed seeing him and talking to him. Link knew another reason why he liked Annie. She treated him as an equal. No hero worship for her. Which, in a way, was a shame. With Diane, he wanted distance. With Annie, he wanted to be closer. Much, much closer.

The doorbell rang, and he understood Annie's plan. "Someone's here," he said to Diane. "I've got to get off the phone . . . No, it's all right. It's someone I was expecting."

He was hanging up the phone when Annie came back into the kitchen. He gave her a thumbs-up. "Worked perfectly," he said. "She could hear the doorbell and believed my excuse that I had to get off."

"So did she call the doctor's office?" Annie began putting away groceries.

"Yes. I guess she's been calling all over the place looking for me. My uncle asked her to." Link shook his head. "The man is getting worse than a mother hen, but I guess I do need to get hold of him and let him know I'm all right."

❖━━━━━━━━❖

It was close to ten o'clock that night when Link finally called his uncle. He wasn't surprised Ron sounded groggy when he answered the phone. Link figured, in Rome, it wasn't quite seven in the morning. As his uncle chastised him for not calling before, Link scraped some of the dead skin off his right leg. Finally, when Ron paused, Link tried to explain. "I did try to call a couple times, but you were either out or the hotel said you hadn't arrived."

Link continued working on his leg as he listened to his uncle's response. Annie had told him that his leg would look terrible when the cast came off, but he hadn't been prepared for the flaking skin. His right leg, from midthigh down, looked as if it belonged to a scrawny-muscled ape with a bad case of dandruff.

"All right, I should have called more often," he said when he got the chance. "I just got so involved with the fuel cell—"

His uncle interrupted him, and Link smiled. Ron was really interested in how he was coming with the fuel cell. "It's looking great," Link said. "Dan Zura's bringing a car over to Annie's in a couple of days and we're going to run some tests, but I think it's ready to go."

When his uncle repeated Annie's name, Link realized he'd basically said where he was. Not that it really mattered. His uncle was in Rome. Link didn't think Ron would be running into many people who even knew he had a nephew, much less cared.

"Yeah, I've been staying with her," he admitted, then laughed at his uncle's next comment. "I wish, but no, we're not sleeping together, so don't get your hopes up. Look, I'll give you the number here, so next time you're worried, just call me. But remember, another four days, if all goes well, I'll be on my way to Detroit."

Two days later Link called to Annie. "Come on out."

The excitement in his voice was unmistakable, and she wiped her hands on a towel, leaving the rest of the carrots to be peeled later. After quickly brushing her fingers through her hair, she headed for the garage.

Dan Zura had arrived earlier that day and had been working with Link on the test car. They now had the garage door up, and she could see the two men leaning over the hood of the car, looking at the engine. Originally a battery-operated EV, the car was even smaller than her Geo, though not by much.

She smiled at the view she was getting of the two men. Both had on shorts: Link's blue and Dan's black. Even if she hadn't known that, she could have recognized Link. His right leg still showed the effects of having been encased in a cast for six weeks. From midthigh down, the leg was paler in color, hairy and thin. She'd been working with him to build the muscles back up, and he was showing progress—he now walked with barely a limp—but she knew its shrunken size bothered him. His vanity amused her. In so many ways he was like her brother and Dennis.

So why was she in love with Link? It was a question she knew she'd never be able to answer.

He glanced her way, then straightened and stepped back from the car. His gray T-shirt had a smudge of dirt across the front, and there was a similar mark on his left cheek. He looked like a little boy playing with his toy car. Then again, there really was nothing boyish about Link Sheffield. He was all man, doing his "man" thing, and now he was showing off his prize. She prepared herself to ooh and aah, as she knew he expected.

"How would you like to take it for a test drive?" he asked.

"Me?" The question startled her, not at all what *she'd* expected.

Dan shut the hood and turned toward her. "It's working fine," he said, grinning. "Our man has done it."

"You want me to test-drive your fuel cell?" She couldn't believe she was going to get the chance. Neither her father nor her brother would have asked her to do something like that. And certainly not Dennis. Cars, in their opinion, were the man's realm.

"Why not?" Link walked over to open the car door for her. "You worked on it just as much as Dan and I." He waited until she got up close, then added, grinning, "Just don't wrap *this* car around any trees."

If he could joke about it, Annie thought, then he didn't blame her for what had happened to his Jaguar. Of course, the fact that his Jag had been repaired and was waiting for him at the dealer's helped. She playfully poked him in the ribs, then looked inside the test car and back at him. "Anything besides trees that I should be aware of?"

"We did it." Link clinked his juice glass against hers, then took a long swallow of champagne.

Dan had brought the bottle but had left before they'd opened it, insisting they celebrate without him. Link had a feeling Dan thought he'd be in the way. He'd tried to explain that he had nothing going on with Annie. All he'd gotten from Dan was a wink and "Then go for it."

If only he dared.

Annie had apologized for not having suitable glasses, but that didn't matter. He wasn't much of a drinker to begin with, especially not of champagne. But a celebration did seem appropriate. Almost seven weeks ago he'd thought his dream had been destroyed. Now it was efficiently powering a car and might possibly be powering a fleet of cars in a year or so. "Next step," he said. "Detroit and the competition."

"I expect more champagne when you win," Annie said.

He liked her positive attitude. No "if you win," but "when." He watched her down half of her champagne, then close her eyes.

They were in the middle of her living room, the air conditioner he'd fixed circulating cool air. Annie was wearing shorts and a T-shirt, one of her loose-fitting shirts similar to all the others she'd started wearing after the incident with her halter and his near seduction. If she thought, however, that she was any less alluring wearing oversized T-shirts, she was mistaken. Link knew from experience that no loose-fitting shirt or air conditioner would cool his thoughts.

Everything about her excited him, from her disheveled hair to her seductive voice. She'd threatened to kick him out of her house if he didn't behave himself, and for five weeks he'd behaved himself, had controlled the urge to touch her when she walked by, had even pretended he wasn't aroused when she reached for something and drew her top tight across her breasts. He'd told himself he could control his desires, though he had to admit, the night he ran into her in the kitchen, when she had on that crazy hot pink nightshirt with the fish and looked so sexy, he'd wanted to grab her and drag her back to his bed. Feigning disinterest that night had not been easy.

In his opinion, his behavior these last five weeks had been exemplary. A monk couldn't have been prouder. But he was tired of being a monk, tired of following her edict, and tired of pretending he didn't want her.

He put down his glass and stepped closer.

Annie opened her eyes and looked up at him, smiling dreamily. "I don't drink champagne very often," she said, her smile captured in her eyes and turning them a sparkling blue.

"Are you going to go and get drunk on me?" He had a feeling she'd be cute drunk, all giggly and silly.

"What would you do if I did?"

"Seduce you."

Her eyes widened at his answer, then her smile turned seductive. "Maybe I'll get drunk then."

He took hope from her response and eased her glass from her hand, setting it on a nearby end table. "Let's not and say you did."

She watched him walk toward her, and he held his breath, waiting for her protest. Stopping in front of her, he reached out and touched her, brushing his fingers over her cheek. Her smile stayed, her gaze never leaving his face. Tentatively, he ran his thumb over her lips, feeling the moisture from the champagne.

"I want you to know how much I appreciate everything you've done," he said, wishing he knew the right words to use. "I feel guilty for completely disrupting your life."

"You have been paying me," she said, cocking her head slightly as if trying to understand where this conversation was headed. "Paying me quite well, in fact."

"You're worth it. I know I'm not an easy man to be around, Annie. When I'm working on something, I get totally involved. And I do tend to be grouchy . . . and grumbly, as you've so often pointed out."

"And you don't like people fussing over you," she added.

"No fussing. You've done everything I've asked, which is why I've felt I had to pay you the same respect."

"Respect is nice."

She wasn't making it easy for him. "What I mean is—" He stared up at the ceiling and blew out a frustrated breath, then looked back at her. Maybe there was a suave way to say it, but he didn't know how. "I want you, Annie. I want to make love with you, to take you to bed and ravish your body. And if you don't want me to, I think you'd better kick me out of this house tonight."

She held his gaze, her expression telling him nothing, then she frowned. "Where would you go?"

His hopes crashed, and he stepped back from her. "I don't know. A motel, I guess."

She shook her head and wrinkled her nose in the cute way he loved. "I don't think you'd like that."

He knew he wouldn't, but he wouldn't push himself on her. "It's your call. You made the rules."

"Link Sheffield, when have you played by the rules?"

"For the last seven weeks," he muttered, not sure if she was telling him to stay or to go. "Dammit, do you want to make love with me or not?"

"You're getting grumbly and grouchy again." She closed her eyes and took in a deep breath. "I should tell you to go."

He turned and started for the door, not quite sure how he would get to a motel since his car was in Oakland. He hadn't taken two steps before Annie called after him. "Where are you going?"

Stopping, he looked back. "You told me to go."

Shaking her head, she walked toward him. "No, I said I should tell you to go." She stopped in front of him. "Geez, you really believe in making it difficult for a woman, don't you?"

Link wasn't quite sure he understood her logic, but the sinking feeling in his stomach disappeared. "What can I say? I'm damned if I do and damned if I don't."

"Then you might as well do, right?" She slipped her arms around his neck, rising up on her toes as she did. "Kiss me, you fool," she ordered, her body fitting perfectly against his.

"Oh, Annie." He did what she asked, pressing his lips against hers, tasting the lingering champagne and the wonder of her. He kissed her and wrapped his arms around her and held her close, breathing in the scent of her. He was a fool. He should have done this a long, long time ago.

"You can't believe how much I've wanted you," he murmured against her mouth. "You've been driving me crazy."

"I didn't know." She had her fingers in his hair. "I had no idea. I thought—"

He heard her sigh of pleasure when he slid his hand between them, rubbing his palm over one breast. "How could you think I didn't want you?" he asked, playing little kisses over her cheek. "I told you I did."

"When?"

"That afternoon in your kitchen. The day I kissed you."

"Link, that was four weeks ago. Almost five."

"So?" He blew into her ear and slipped his hand down over her abdomen, feeling her suck in her breath. "Did you really think I'd changed my mind?"

"Yes. I mean, I thought—" She didn't finish, and he knew it didn't matter. The past was the past. The present was another matter.

She leaned her head back, and he kissed her exposed throat, licking her skin with the tip of his tongue. He could feel her heat, hear her ragged breathing. He knew his was as ragged as hers. "Where shall we go, your room or mine?" he asked, knowing he wasn't going to last long. His foreplay had gone on for seven weeks. From the very beginning she'd excited him.

"My bed's bigger," she said, easing herself away from his body.

"And bigger is better. Right?"

She gave him a quick look as she headed toward her bedroom. "That sounds like a male thing. I've seen yours. Remember?"

"Didn't seem quite fair to me," he said, keeping up with her. "You've seen mine, but I haven't seen yours." He caught her hand, stopping her before she stepped into her bedroom. "I need to get something. I'll be there in a moment." He let his glance travel down her front. "Why don't you slip out of something comfortable?"

TWELVE

With a small whimper, she gave herself to me, her mouth ripe and succulent. I ran my hand down the naked expanse of her torso until my fingers reached the waistband of her shorts. I could smell the fragrant heat of her body. . . .

—The Dancer

Annie cleared off her bed and pulled back her comforter. Her thoughts were chaotic, her emotions frenzied. It would be nice to blame her actions on the champagne, but she knew what she was doing. Well, at least she hoped she did.

Link had given her a choice, except she'd gone beyond the point of deciding. She'd hoped she could control her feelings for him by keeping their relationship platonic. Over and over, while lying in bed by herself, longing for him, she'd told herself what she was doing was wise and for the best. She'd even partially convinced herself that once he was gone, she would be able to go on with her life as she had before. But now, as the time for him to leave for Detroit was drawing near, she knew it was all a lie.

Denying her desires had been a mistake. She was in love with Link and when he left, he was going to take a part of her heart with him, whether they made love or not. Once he was gone, all she would have were the memories. She didn't want to be left wishing she had one more memory.

She stared at the flowered sheet that covered her mattress and the two pillows with their matching cases, then realized she wasn't alone. Link stood in the doorway to her bedroom, watching her, his warm smile touching her as no words could. He was still wearing the gray T-shirt with the smudge of dirt and his blue shorts, but he'd kicked off his shoes. She did the same, slinging hers toward her closet but not really caring where they landed. "Did you get what you needed?" she asked, suddenly feeling very shy.

"I did." He walked into the room and lay a handful of foil packets on the table by her bed.

She glanced at them, then at him. "It's going to be a long night."

"I figured it was better to be prepared." He glanced at her shirt, then looked down at his own. Quickly he pulled off his, letting it fall at his feet.

She watched him come near. A smattering of dark hairs covered his chest, trailing down to a thin line that disappeared beneath the waistline of his shorts. "Nervous?" he asked, and she realized her gaze had dropped to his hips.

Quickly she looked back up. "Who, me? Why would I be nervous? It's not like we don't know each other."

"This is different." He stopped directly in front of her and combed his fingers through her hair, drawing it back from her face, then letting it fall forward again. In his eyes she saw a look that warmed her to her toes, and she felt sexy, desired, and wanted.

Suddenly she *was* nervous.

"I'm, ah, not very experienced at this." If he was expecting a consummate lover, he was going to be disappointed. "I haven't slept with many men, and my husband certainly wasn't impressed."

"Hush." Link touched a fingertip to her lips, silencing her. "This is between you and me, no one else."

He drew her up on her toes and kissed her lightly, almost pensively, then he pulled back and looked down at her. "Annie, is that what you've been afraid of, that I might be disappointed?"

"I—" How she wished she could tell him her fears. How she wished she could make him love her as she loved him. But she knew that was impossible and merely shrugged in answer.

"Don't be," he said. "If anyone's going to be disappointed, it's going to be you."

"I don't think so."

"God, I hope not, because I want you so badly."

He kissed her again, the tenderness and hesitancy gone. Kissed and touched her, taking off her T-shirt, then her bra. With the palms of his hands, he cradled her breasts, adoring them with his eyes before kissing each. He sucked at her nipples, creating swirls of moisture with his tongue as he stroked and caressed her body until she was burning for more. A giddy sensation curled through her when he pushed down her shorts, dropping them to the floor, and between her legs muscles tightened, aching to be stretched. She wanted him inside of her, filling her and becoming a part of her.

He eased her back on the bed, and she watched with half-closed eyes as he slipped off her panties, then took off his shorts and boxer shorts. For a moment he simply stared at her, then he touched her, his fingertips brushing her between her legs and sending a shock of excitement from her hips on up. And when he slid a finger inside her, she knew he found her wet and ready. Yet she wasn't prepared for her reaction when he began gently stroking her with his fingers. In an instant, pleasure turned to tremors of need, and she knew if Link didn't stop, she was going to explode into a thousand pieces.

She cried out his name, and he smiled, then leaned toward the nightstand. One foil packet was retrieved and opened, and he sat back, giving her full view of his hips. She'd seen him naked before, had bathed him and helped him to go to the bathroom. She knew him intimately, yet this was far more intimate.

Ready, he leaned close and kissed her, the hairs on his chest brushing her nipples and sending tingles of excitement spiraling down her belly. "Just looking at you," he began, "I—"

He didn't finish. The time for words was over. Link eased himself over her, spreading her legs with his knees. Annie felt him press against her, tentatively at first. Cautiously. Her body opened to him, and she felt him thrust.

Suddenly he was inside of her, and though she tried, she couldn't help the small cry that escaped her.

Immediately Link stopped, his expression concerned.

"I'm okay, keep going," she pleaded, amazed by how good he did feel. "It's just been a while."

He withdrew and again pressed himself into her, more carefully this time, and she felt herself easily accepting him. Taking him in and surrounding him. They were one, linked by a desire that had been growing every day, brought together by a chemistry she didn't understand and a love she couldn't control. His need was hers.

He paused for a moment and kissed her. "You feel wonderful," he said.

She hadn't realized how much she'd needed his reassurance or how heavy the weight of self-doubt had been. Maybe they were only words, but they meant so much. "So do you," she said with a sigh. "So do you."

She touched his arms, feeling the tension in his muscles. He was poised and ready, and so was she. He made her feel beautiful and sexy, made her want to give him pleasure. "Love me, Link," she murmured. "Be wild. Be savage. Be a conquering warrior."

He laughed, the sound deep and guttural. "I think you've got the wrong man."

Looking deep into his eyes, his wonderful, intelligent, beautiful eyes, she shook her head. "Not at all. I've got exactly the right man."

"I hope so," he said softly, then began to move, his thrusts tentative at first, exploratory.

She knew exactly when Link Sheffield, teacher and inventor, lost control. His rhythm changed first, quickening with each thrust. The driving of his hips grew harder, deeper, and more demanding. A sheen of sweat covered his body, and his breathing turned harsh.

She wasn't sure she was breathing at all and the sound of her heartbeat was thundering in her ears. He was creating a pressure she wanted released, pushing her toward a point of no return and driving her crazy. She grasped his shoulders, clinging to him for support, knowing he would probably come before she did, if she made it at all. It was always that way for her: the promise of ecstasy so close, yet so far away. Only later, if he cared enough to take the time, would he be able to bring her satisfaction. She was willing to—

It happened. Slamming through her, her climax came forcefully, utterly consuming her. She heard herself saying yes, over and over, heard her groans, and knew she'd never experienced anything like it before.

It wasn't until a delicious, relaxing pleasure flowed through her that she realized Link had been holding himself still to allow her to fully enjoy what was happening. Blinking open her eyes, she saw his satisfied smile and knew that wasn't entirely true. He'd taken pleasure in her pleasure. "Wow," she said, no word adequate for what she'd experienced.

"Double wow," he said, and began to move again.

His thrusts were rapid and deep, his concentration focused, and she knew the moment he found his climax. Arching his back, he threw back his head and cried out. Male and arrogant, he claimed his victory. He was truly the conquerer, the master. Yet when he looked down at her and smiled again, she knew they were both the winners, and she would treasure this moment for a lifetime.

During the night, her cat joined them on the bed. Ziggy curled up beside her, as he always did, but when Link woke her, some time after midnight, and began kissing her, Ziggy moved to the end of the bed.

Annie had to rescue the cat when Link flung the sheet back, the heat of their renewed lovemaking making any covering unbearable. Ziggy jumped off the bed with a disgruntled, complaining yowl, and Annie knew he didn't share her enthusiasm for making love throughout the night. She, however, liked it just fine.

In the morning, there were four fewer foil packets on the nightstand, and she felt thoroughly loved. Lying beside Link, she knew she'd made a mistake keeping him out of her bed. "Boy, did I waste six weeks," she murmured to herself.

Link's chuckle beside her told her he'd heard. "I tried to tell you."

"Some things I just have to learn for myself." Except she'd wasted too much time learning, and soon he would be gone. She turned her head on the pillow so she was looking at Link. "When do you leave for Detroit?"

He smiled. "Don't worry. We have one more night. I'm not going until tomorrow."

One more night. It was too little time. And then he would be gone, out of her life, and as far as Lois Greenman would know, Annie's aunt in Peoria would suddenly get better, and Annie would resume her life as it had been before, going from home to home, offering nursing care. And Dr. Link Sheffield would have accomplished his goal, would have his wonderful, revolutionary fuel cell in the competition. There was only one hitch. "What about the attempts on your life?"

"Well, I'm not going to stay in hiding for the rest of my life. It was one thing staying here until my leg was healed and the fuel cell finished, but either the police have got to figure out who planted that bomb and cut the brake lines or I'm going to."

And he would, she knew, even if it cost him his life. "This isn't a mystery novel," she said, quoting what he'd once said to her. "In real life the good guy doesn't always win. You can't just go running around looking for the bad guy. You could get hurt. Killed."

"You're fussing, Annie."

"Well, maybe someone needs to fuss over you."

He touched a fingertip to her lips. "I'll be okay. I'm a big boy. I'm not going to do anything foolish."

Before she could speak, he kissed her, and she knew how foolish she'd been to fall in love with him. She also felt the hard length of his shaft bump against her hip, and knew he wanted her again. Grinning, she glanced down at his erection. "My, my, you *are* a big boy."

"Want to try for five?"

Ziggy jumped back on the bed at eight o'clock, gave Link a disdainful look, and walked over him to reach Annie. When the cat gave a plaintive meow, she stroked his head, soothing him with words. Link simply watched, fascinated by the exchange between animal and human. Annie spoke, and the cat answered, or so it seemed. And it seemed that Annie understood what the cat said. Sitting up, she looked at Link. "He's hungry. After I feed him, I'll put some coffee on." She smiled. "And yes, I'll make it strong and black."

"See that you do," he said, mocking his attitude when she'd first come to care for him. Then he gave her butt a pat. "Then come back and take care of my other needs."

"Oh, yeah?" She stepped away from the bed, and he noticed she didn't show any shyness in being naked. He liked that, liked having her open and honest with him. She wrinkled her nose and shook her head. "You are insatiable."

She did slip on her shorts and a top before she left the bedroom, and he watched her every movement, knowing she was right. Where she was concerned, he was insatiable. He wanted to be near her, to touch her, to listen to her talk and laugh, and to make love with her. He didn't know what he was going to do when he left. For two months she'd been a part of his life. He'd been married to Marian for two years before she left, but what he felt for Annie was different from what he'd ever felt for Marian. With Annie there was more than the sex. More than living together and doing things together. She'd become his friend and his companion. For two months, he'd depended on her for everything.

He stared at the ceiling and knew what lay ahead. He had to leave. In the last two months, he'd become too dependent on Annie. He was asking for a heartache. Ultimately she would leave. It always happened.

Link was working in the garage when the doorbell rang. Annie answered it. "Is there a Link Sheffield living here?" a man in a gray uniform asked, a package in his hands.

"Yes." She frowned. No one was supposed to know Link was at her house.

The deliveryman held the package toward her. "This is for him. I was supposed to get it here this morning, but my truck broke down."

"That's for Link?" She glanced at the package. It was about the size of a shirt box and wrapped in brown paper. She saw no store logo, and the sign on the white van parked in front of her place simply said VALLEY DELIVERY. "Who sent this?"

The deliveryman looked at a clipboard he held. "Someone named . . ." He frowned. "Zurr, maybe?"

"Zura," Annie said, sighing with relief. If the package was from Dan, everything made sense. "Thanks."

The box weighed more than she'd expected. She thanked the delivery man, but if he was expecting a tip, he didn't get one. After closing the door, she headed straight for the garage. Link was working on his fuel cell, tinkering with wires and concentrating on what he was doing. She knew he probably hadn't heard the doorbell and wasn't aware of her presence in the doorway. She cleared her throat before speaking, and he looked up. "A package just arrived for you."

His frown was immediate. "What package?"

"This package." She held it up for him to see. "Dan sent it."

"Dan? What's Dan sending me? Looks like a box of candy."

She gave the box a slight shake and shook her head. "Feels heavier than candy."

Link glanced down at the fuel cell, then back at her. "I'm busy right now. Can you open it?"

"Sure. That's what assistants are for, isn't it?"

He smiled at her, and she started to tear at the paper on one end. Her efforts were interrupted by the ringing of the telephone. "Assistants also answer phones," she said, and headed for the kitchen, carrying the package with her. She set it on the kitchen table and answered the phone.

For a moment there was no response, then a woman hesitantly asked if Link was there. Annie frowned. "Who is this?"

Immediately the caller hung up.

"Who was that?" Link asked from the doorway to the laundry room.

Annie turned toward him, concerned and confused. "I don't know. It was a woman . . . asking for you."

He shook his head and walked into the room. At the table he stopped and looked at the package she'd set down, then he headed for her, snagging an arm around her waist and holding her close. "I don't like this," he said. "I don't like it at all."

He picked up the phone and dialed a number. Annie leaned against him, afraid she knew what Link was thinking. She was right. Dan Zura told Link he hadn't sent anything.

Link's next call was to Detective Bronson.

The local police came, along with Detective Bronson and a bomb squad. Link had decided he wasn't taking any chances. If he was wrong, he'd wasted an hour that he could have spent working on the fuel cell, and had worked up a sweat for nothing. On the other hand, pushing the EV with the fuel cell in it out of the garage had been good exercise, and standing around on the front lawn, playing with the cat and talking to Annie wasn't all bad. He'd even had a chance to meet Annie's neighbor, Mrs. Moore, a nosey old lady who reminded him of his grandmother, except Mrs. Moore didn't have bad breath. Still she did fuss, bringing them lemonade to drink and cookies to eat.

Detective Bronson made notes, quizzing Annie about the deliveryman and the phone call. "Did you recognize the caller's voice?" he asked her.

"I don't think so. She really didn't say that much, just asked if Link was here, then hung up when I asked who it was."

"Do you think it was Diane?" Link asked.

"I don't know." Annie looked at him. "I wondered that myself. But how would she get my number?"

He grimaced. "I might have given it to her. I called her from here. If she has one of those caller ID systems, it would have shown your number."

They watched as the bomb squad came out of Annie's

house, the package now in a container. Bronson walked over and spoke to one of the officers, then returned to them. "They'll check the package, X-ray it, then let me know what they find. Once I know, I'll call you." He nodded toward the house. "You'll be here?"

"If you think it's safe." Link wasn't sure now.

The officer standing next to Bronson spoke up. "We'll have a man drive by every two hours, but if anything suspicious happens, call 911."

The call from Bronson came nearly three hours later. Link listened, asked a couple of questions and made a few comments, then hung up and returned to the kitchen table where Annie was sitting. She waited, knowing from his expression that it wasn't good news. Finally he spoke. "It was a bomb. It was rigged so the moment you opened it, it would have gone off."

He hesitated, and Annie remembered how she'd shaken the box and how close she'd come to opening it. She had a feeling Link was also remembering. "Does Bronson have any idea who sent it?"

"He says there's a fingerprint. It's the first real lead. He wants to tap your phone. He thinks this woman might call back. I told him I'd talk to you, but that you'd probably agree."

"Certainly," she said.

"I've been thinking—" He paused and scooted his chair closer, taking her hands in his. "I've got to leave tomorrow. If I don't, I may not get the fuel cell to Detroit in time. But why don't you come with me? Let the police tap your phone. We could also connect a caller ID and make a tape recording of your voice. I can set it all up so that if this woman calls again, the tape would be activated. She'd think she had you, her number would be recorded, and the police would have something. It would actually be better than depending on getting a trace."

Annie only partially followed what he was saying about the tape and caller ID. It was what he'd said in the beginning that had caught her attention. "You want me to go with you . . . to Detroit?"

"Yes." He looked at her as if it were an obvious move. "I don't want you staying here, not by yourself."

"What about Ziggy?" She glanced at her cat, curled under the table.

"Leave him with Mrs. Moore. You've done it before. We'll be gone a week or so. By then, Bronson should have something."

He seemed to have it all planned. She wasn't sure, however, that going to Detroit with him was a good idea. She'd come to accept that her time with Link was about to end. For the last few days she'd been preparing herself for his departure. She'd actually convinced herself that she was ready for him to leave.

And now?

Now he was suggesting she go along, spend the next week to ten days with him.

Annie played the idea over in her mind. On the positive side, going with him would mean more time to love him and be loved by him. On the negative side, he would still leave her. But would his leaving hurt any more in ten days than it would if he left that night? Could she love him any more a week from now than she already did? She didn't see how.

What life was offering her was a gift, a gift of time.

She grinned up at him. "How long do I have to get things packed and ready? And what do I need to bring?"

Later that night, they were on their way to her bedroom when the phone rang. Annie stopped where she was and stared back toward the kitchen. Link decided it was time he stopped hiding. He walked back to the kitchen, picked up the phone, and spoke into it.

A cold chill ran down his spine when no one answered. He knew someone was on the line. Someone who was listening. "Hello," he repeated, glancing down at the caller ID box they'd connected that afternoon.

A click was his response, and he hung up the phone and faced Annie.

The color was gone from her cheeks, her eyes expressing her fear. He wanted to reassure her, to tell her that everything would be all right. All he could do was shake his head.

THIRTEEN

"Talk to me," she screamed into the mouthpiece. "Say something."

The silence was terrifying, and she slammed down the telephone. For a moment she stood there, staring at it, her heart pounding in her ears. She knew what was coming next.

The phone rang.

—Don't Cry Wolf

"It was her, wasn't it?" Annie said, tasting a fear she'd never known before.

"I don't know." Link walked from the phone to where she stood. "Whoever it was knew enough to block their phone number so it wouldn't show up on the caller ID."

She stepped into his embrace, needing his comfort. She was scared. "It was her," she said firmly. "She called to—"

The reason why Diane had called was clear, and Annie leaned back to look up at Link. "She called because she wanted to see if you were still alive. But why, Link? Why is she doing this?"

"I don't know." He drew her close to his body and nuzzled his face in her hair. "Honey, we don't even know for sure that it is Diane."

"Who else could it be?"

"Maybe that call had nothing to do with what's been going on. Maybe someone just dialed a wrong number, realized his mistake, and hung up."

"Are you going to tell me you really believe that?"

He shook his head. "Do you want to go somewhere tonight? Somewhere safe? A motel?"

She thought about it, then decided against the idea. "No. What I want to do is get some sleep and get out of here as early as we can tomorrow. I don't know why someone's trying to kill you, but I'll feel safer when we're far, far away from here."

"Annie?"

She looked up at him. He was staring down at her with an odd expression, then he closed his eyes and kissed the top of her head. "Thank you," was all he said.

They made love. Annie knew she needed the physical contact, and from the way Link kissed her and held her, she sensed his fears were the same as hers, though he refused to admit them. He was so like her father and brother. He was even like Dennis. Yet Link was different from all three of them. She knew him now, knew his grumbling and grouching were a front, that all she had to do was stand up to him and he would back down. She knew he was afraid she would leave him, as so many had left him. What she didn't know was if he loved her.

He hadn't said and she hadn't asked. She was afraid to ask, afraid he might say no.

Sleep came quickly to her once Link stretched out beside her, his needs and hers both met. The night before had taken its toll, along with the events of the day. She decided she'd much rather read mysteries than be a part of one. The heroes and heroines could live life on the edge. She'd rather experience it vicariously, safely curled up on her couch.

Annie pushed the cat away and grumbled groggily. All she wanted to do was sleep. She was tired. So tired.

Again Ziggy bumped her face with his. His plaintive cry was different from usual. Worried.

Desperate.

She pushed him away.

Link grunted, and she heard him mumble something that sounded like "Damn cat." She knew then that she was going to have to do something, put Ziggy out of the room and close the door. Groaning, not even opening her eyes, she pushed back the sheet and sat up.

Immediately she began coughing.

Smoke filled her nostrils, burned her throat, and infiltrated her lungs. She coughed and coughed, her eyes snapping open. In the darkness she couldn't see a thing, yet she knew it was there, hanging around her head and burning her eyes. Smoke—heavy, thick, and deadly. In the distance, she heard something crackling and snapping, then down the hallway she saw the glow.

"Fire," she gasped, and dropped back down below the layer of smoke to where the air was still pure.

She pushed on Link's shoulders. He grumbled, and she knew she didn't have time to explain. "Get out of bed," she ordered. "Stay low. The house is on fire. We've got to get out."

Link came awake with a jolt, sat up, and gagged, then dropped back down to the bed, rolling off the edge as he did. He was naked and for a moment couldn't remember where he'd tossed his shorts. Feeling around on the floor, he found them. He heard Annie call for her cat, then the bedroom door shut. His shorts on, he crawled around the bed to where he'd last heard her. By the time he reached the end of the bed, there was a sound at the window. She was pushing it up.

She swore, and he hurried to her side. "I can't get the screen off," she said, panic in her voice.

"Let me." He felt along the edges, then decided to forget releasing it. With a punch of his fist he took it out, then turned to her. "You go first."

He could tell from the streetlights that she had the cat in her arms. He helped her climb out, then followed, the dew-wet grass cool beneath his feet. He sucked in cool, fresh air, coughed and gagged, and watched the smoke billow out into the night. Flames were rising from the middle of the house, devouring it with frightening speed.

"Here, take him," Annie said, and thrust her cat into his arms. Before he could say anything, she was off at a run, dashing toward the garage.

Holding on to the cat, he followed, his recently broken leg stiff and slowing him down. He saw her push up the garage door, and he yelled at her. At the same time a neighbor came out of his house and yelled at him. Vaguely Link registered that the fire department had been called. He didn't care. Seeing Annie go into the garage, his only thought was to get her out.

Smoke filled the garage, Annie's form indiscernible. Mrs. Moore had stepped out of the house next door, her robe wrapped tight around her. She stood near the driveway, staring at the burning house. Link thrust the cat into her arms and headed for the garage.

Annie came out just as he started in. In her arms were his papers, the notes and sketches he'd been making for the last seven weeks. The pile had been scattered around in the garage. For her to have gone in after them was insane.

The moment she reached him, she released the breath she'd been holding, then began coughing and choking. She handed the papers to him and bent over, gagging and trying to draw in fresh air. He looked at the papers, then dropped them on the driveway and tried to help her. But she was shaking her head, motioning toward the papers.

"Don't let them . . ." She coughed. "Get blown away. Your notes . . ." She motioned toward the truck parked in the drive. They'd rented it that afternoon and had already packed the fuel cell in it. "We've got to move . . . that."

Still coughing from the smoke she'd inhaled, she started for the truck. Link knew he either had to back it up, or she'd try pushing it away from the house. Since he'd left the keys in his shorts pocket, driving seemed the easier alternative. "Get in," he ordered, and grabbing up the papers, headed for the truck himself.

With her seated beside him, he backed the truck out onto the street, parking it a safe distance away from the burning house. The first fire engine was racing down the road by the time they got out of the rental truck. Sirens blazing and lights flashing, it pulled up in front of Annie's house. The flames were now leaping through the roof and eating away at everything in their path. Smoke had been replaced by fire in the garage, and Link knew if Annie hadn't gotten his papers out, they would have been destroyed.

Together, they stood by Mrs. Moore. Annie had reclaimed her cat, holding him close and praising him for waking them. The cat only wanted to get away, and Link suggested she take him into Mrs. Moore's house.

When Annie came back out, the fire was nearly extinguished. Three big fire trucks blocked the front of her house and two police cars were parked beside their rental truck. Link was talking to the officers and Annie joined him. He glanced at her when she approached, then slipped an arm around her shoulders. "This is the owner of the house," he said, introducing her to the officers. "It was her cat that alerted us to the fire."

It was after three o'clock in the morning when the fire department was finished. Detective Bronson arrived at about the same time, looking tired and rumpled. One of Annie's neighbors had made coffee and was carrying a thermos of it and foam cups around, giving it to anyone who wanted some. Bronson gladly accepted a cup, took a long swallow, then set the cup on the fender of the rental truck, pulled out his notebook, and began asking questions.

They were the same questions the local police officers had asked, but Annie knew Bronson would see this as a part of a whole rather than as a simple fire. He'd already picked up information from the fire chief. "Fire started along the back of your house. Definitely arson. The section near your bedroom didn't catch as rapidly as the section near the living room, which is lucky for you two. Looks like he cut through a screen in the living room, opened a window, and poured the accelerant on your drapes there."

"You're sure it was a man?" Annie asked.

Bronson shook his head. "No. We still don't have an ID on that fingerprint we took from the bomb. Maybe there are some footprints around here—" He looked down at the ground and shook his head. "Chances are we won't find anything."

Annie could understand why not. Dozens of people had trampled over the area, firefighters, the police, and even neighbors. If the arsonist had left footprints, they would be hard to distinguish among all the others.

"One thing, however," Bronson said, closing his notebook and slipping it back into the inside pocket of his jacket. "Whoever is doing this is getting sloppy. The first try on your life, Dr. Sheffield, was very professional. Even the cut brakes might have been missed if you'd been in an accident. But the bomb this afternoon and this fire to-night, well . . ."

He glanced at the house. Smoldering timbers were all that remained of the garage and center portion of the structure. The two bedrooms, bathroom, and hallway had been spared, but Annie knew the water the firefighters had poured into those rooms had damaged everything. That and the smoke. If she hadn't been so scared, she might be depressed.

Detective Bronson looked back at them. "Also, the first attack didn't seem to be aimed at you, Dr. Sheffield. I mean, you said yourself that you usually didn't go to the lab at night. That bomb was set for eleven-thirty. I think your being there when it went off was merely a chance event."

"That is," Annie said, "*if* the bomb was timed to go off at eleven-thirty."

"That's what the experts tell me." Bronson picked up his cup of coffee again, took a sip, and grimaced. "Cold," he said and poured the rest onto the drive, letting it blend with the water still rushing from the house.

"Even the cut brakes might not have resulted in your death. An accident, yes. And you did experience one. Not a bad one, but an accident. Which, I think, was supposed to be a warning to you. But you obviously didn't heed the warning, because this last bomb and this fire are showing more desperation on our perpetrator's part." He glanced at the charred house. "There is definitely something you're doing that this person doesn't want you doing."

"My uncle thinks it's the fuel cell I'm working on,"

Link said, and glanced at Annie. "That's why he didn't want me working on it. He was worried for my safety."

"Makes sense," Bronson said. "The fuel cell was in the lab during that first explosion, right? That one was completely destroyed, if I recall."

"Along with his notes," Annie added.

"And the accident with your car happened after you decided to make another fuel cell?"

"That's right," Link said.

"And who knew you were working on another one?"

Link hesitated for a moment, then answered. "Four people knew. Five if you include Annie. There was Jeff Yamaguchi. He's the former student and assistant who came to my house after the explosion. Since he encouraged me to get back to work on the fuel cell, it seems doubtful he'd be trying to stop me from working on it. Then there's Dan Zura. He's been helping me with this one. In fact, he was out just yesterday."

Bronson pulled his notebook back out. "This is the Dan Zura who supposedly sent the package with the bomb?"

"Yes, but he said he never sent anything. If he wanted me out of the way, he could have said nothing, we would have opened the package, and—"

Bronson nodded. "Boom. Doesn't sound like he'd be the one, but it could be he knew you'd call and only wanted to scare you, so we've got to keep him in mind. The other two?" He glanced toward Annie. "Besides Annie."

"Diane Wilson," Annie said, picking up where Link

had left off. "His assistant up until after the first explosion."

"Ah, yes." Bronson turned to a previous page in his notebook. "The assistant whose briefcase held the original bomb."

"Who couldn't have been involved because she was on a cruise when that bomb went off," Link reminded them.

"She could have set it up before she left," Annie said.

"She's right," Bronson added. "You don't know when that briefcase was put into place. It was a digital timer. It could have been set days ahead of time."

"Diane was still on that cruise when Annie heard someone near my car," Link argued.

"But we don't know if the noise I heard that night was actually when your brakes were cut." Annie knew Link didn't want to believe Diane could do such a thing, but she wasn't as sure.

"Okay, that makes three," Bronson said. "Who's the fourth person who knew you were back working on the fuel cell?"

"Just my uncle. But he's in Europe. He hasn't been around since right after that first explosion. That's why Annie was hired in the first place."

"So it looks like we need to pick up your assistant, Miss—" Bronson glanced at his notebook for Diane's last name.

"Wilson," Link said, shaking his head. "I just can't believe she'd do something like this." He stared at the charred shell of Annie's house.

"Well, maybe she didn't, but she may be able to supply some answers." He again put the notebook away. "When did you say you were leaving for Detroit?"

"In the morning," Annie said, then realized it was morning. "Soon." She patted the side of the truck they were leaning against. "His fuel cell is in here and ready to go." She looked down at her nightshirt. Smudges of soot decorated her psychedelic fish. Then she looked at Link. He was bare-chested and barefoot, his hair rumpled as usual. "We just have to find some clothes to wear."

"I've got some at my place," Link said. "And we can buy you some once the stores open." He looked at Bronson. "Is it safe to go back to my place?"

"We'll make sure it's safe."

At Link's house, they took showers. Link packed clothes for himself, and loaned Annie a T-shirt and a pair of shorts she could wear, though they had to pin the shorts to keep them up on her slim hips. The sun was up by the time they were ready and had what they needed in the rental truck. Exhausted, they climbed in and drove off, neither saying a word. Annie leaned back against the seat and closed her eyes. Images of the last twenty-four hours flashed through her mind. The day before, she'd thought Link would be leaving this morning, had been worried she would never see him again. Now she was going with him, had no house to return to, and was wearing Link's clothes. Life had a way of throwing surprises at a person.

The truck bounced down the winding road, and she wondered how her car had fared. Last she remembered, her neighbors had been pushing it clear of her house. At the time, the welfare of her car had been the least of her concerns.

At the bottom of the hill, Link stopped and Annie opened her eyes. Cars whizzed by, workers on their way to their jobs. She expected him to turn right. He flicked on the left turn signal and glanced her way. "I was thinking," he said. "You got my notes and papers out. If the fuel cell is the cause of all of this, I sort of hate to carry them with it. But I didn't want to leave them at my place. The way things have been going, it may be burned to the ground next. I think I'm going to go by my uncle's place and leave the papers there. It's not that far out of the way, and if anything should happen—"

"Nothing's going to happen," she said, hoping she sounded more positive than she felt. "But I think that's a good idea."

Link parked the truck in front of his uncle's house. The place looked in good shape, but then his uncle had a gardener and cleaning lady who came once a week. Annie stirred beside him. She'd been sleeping for the last half hour. He knew she needed it. They both needed more sleep.

The idea of staying at his uncle's for the day was tempting. No one would know he was there. It would be safe. They could both get the sleep they needed.

Link smiled, his gaze traveling down over Annie's figure. She looked cute in his T-shirt. Sexy. It wasn't sleep he wanted. Making love with Annie was addictive. He couldn't seem to get enough. Surely they had time.

She blinked open her eyes and smiled at him, then sat up and stretched, pulling his shirt tight against her breasts, and he knew he was going to make the time. "We're there," he said. "Come on in with me. I want to show you around."

"Sure," she said, and opened her door.

Although he'd given her a pair of thongs to use until they got her some clothes, she left them in the truck and stood barefoot on the sidewalk, waiting for him as he got his papers, then locked the truck. Slipping an arm around her shoulders, he walked with her to the front door. "I picked up the key while at my place. I have a key to his house and he has a key to mine."

He inserted his key, released the dead bolt, then the lock. "There's an alarm system," he said, starting for the kitchen, then he stopped. "Hmm, that's funny. It's not on. The cleaning lady must have forgotten to set it after she left."

"Link?"

Annie's voice sounded funny, and he turned to see what was the matter. He knew immediately. Standing in the hallway was his uncle, and in Ron Sheffield's hand was a gun.

FOURTEEN

I had the suspects all gathered in the living room, and the scene made me think of the old Charlie Chan movies I'd seen. Now was the time for the detective to explain everything . . . what had happened and who the murderer was. Only problem was, I didn't have the slightest clue what had happened or who had killed the old man.

—Number One Son

"Uncle Ron?" Link said, staring at the gun. "It's me."

"So I see," his uncle said coolly, not lowering the gun.

"I was just going to turn off the security system." Link glanced that way. "But then I realized it wasn't on. I thought maybe the cleaning lady had forgotten to turn it on." He frowned. "What are you doing here?"

"Question is, what are you doing here?" Ron stepped into the foyer, his gaze darting from Annie to Link. Then he smiled. "Looks like you two had a rough night."

Annie might have thought he was being friendly, but

the smile hadn't reached Ron's eyes and he hadn't lowered his gun. It was still pointed at Link. She looked at Link, wondering what he was going to do.

Link himself was looking at the gun, still frowning. With a wave of his hand, he motioned toward the weapon. "What's this?"

"Insurance," Ron said. "Nothing else seems to be working."

Annie closed her eyes, not wanting to believe the thoughts rushing through her mind. This was Link's uncle. Ron Sheffield was the concerned and caring relative. He was Link's only living relative. The polite and courteous Sheffield. He acted like a gentleman.

Except, holding a gun on your nephew wasn't a very gentlemanly act.

Again she looked at him, noting the hard line of his mouth and the intense look in his eyes. This was not the man who'd greeted her at Link's door almost eight weeks ago, who'd been so concerned about his nephew's welfare. The man she was looking at now showed no emotion, and that frightened her.

"You planted the bomb, didn't you?" she said, and he glanced at her. "And you're the one who cut the brake line on Link's car and set the fire."

Again, he smiled, slightly. "Too bad you didn't figure that out before."

"You did all of those things?" Link stared at his uncle. "But why?"

"Why?" Ron looked surprised by the question. "To stop you, of course." He shook his head. "You really shouldn't have built that fuel cell, not this year. Actually, I'm not sure I could have let you build it any year."

He looked at Annie again, as if wanting her to understand. "He's too smart for his own good, you know. I think he gets that from me. His mother, she was stubborn. Stubborn and unpredictable. He's inherited those traits too, I'm afraid." He looked back at Link. "I do love you, though. Love you like my own son."

"Holding a gun on me is a strange way to show it," Link said, taking a step toward his uncle.

"I wouldn't do that," Ron said, and Annie saw him raise the gun so it was pointed right at Link's chest. At this close range, there was no way the man could miss.

She spoke up quickly. "Are you saying that Link is your son?"

Ron shot her a look, and she noticed his hand came down slightly. "Chances are, he is. Rachel said he was, but I don't know for sure. That might just have been to get what she wanted from me. She thought she was so smart, that she could play me against my brother. She shouldn't have tried, you know. She should have divorced Robert when I asked her to and married me. But no, she said he was more stable. She wanted him, and she wanted me."

"Is that why she left, took off?" Annie asked. Even under the circumstances, she thought knowing why his mother had left might help Link deal with Rachel's desertion.

"Left?" Ron smiled. "I guess you could say she left, though she was never really far away." He looked at Link. "Remember that park you used to like to play in? She's there. Under the oak tree. I was afraid they might dig her up when they were talking about turning it into a parking lot. That's why I fought so hard to keep the park as it was. No need to stir up old memories."

"You killed my mother?" Link said, the shock in his expression tearing at Annie's heart. She'd wanted him to know why his mother had left. She hadn't thought he'd learn she'd been killed.

Ron answered as calmly as if he were describing a business deal. "I simply showed her what happens if you go against Ron Sheffield."

"And how is Link going against you?" Annie asked.

"He came up with that fuel cell."

"But how does that hurt you?"

"Well, he knew I'd invested in SunCoast."

"They're making solar-powered engines," Link said. "Not hydrogen-powered EVs."

"Last year they started working on hydrogen-powered EVs," Ron said. "Actually, you're the reason they went into hydrogen power. Jim—" Ron glanced at Annie. "Jim Fisher, he's the president of SunCoast. He and I were having lunch, and I mentioned what Link had told me about that bus up in Vancouver and about Ballard Power. Jim had already been complaining that the solar engine was going nowhere. I suggested he look into hydrogen power. So he did." Ron grinned proudly at Link. "SunCoast has a fuel cell in that EV5 competition. It's good. Very good. I know because I saw it work five months ago. It's so good, I decided to put a little more money into the company." Again, he looked at Annie, as if needing her understanding. "Actually, a lot more. It's a small company. They had to have the capital to get one ready for Detroit."

"Why?" Link asked. "Why did you finance them when you knew I was working on a hydrogen fuel cell?"

"Because, at the time, I didn't know you were working on one," Ron snapped. "When have you ever told me what you're working on?"

The calm that Ron had been displaying was frightening, but for Annie, his temper was even more terrifying. She knew she had to soothe him. "It's been hard on you, hasn't it? Having to take over the business. Knowing it was in financial jeopardy, then having the company you'd invested in also jeopardized."

"Yes," he said, some of the tension leaving his expression. "Not that Sheffield's Tools ever should have been in jeopardy. That was all Link's brother's fault. And my brother's." He shook his head. "Why Robert let Larry make those changes, I don't know. I warned him about them, told him what would happen. But would he listen to me? No."

Annie saw Link close his eyes for a moment and take in a deep breath, and she knew he had come to the same conclusion she had. Link asked the question. "That plane crash," he said. "It wasn't an accident, was it?"

His uncle looked at him, no remorse showing. "I couldn't let them go on the way they were. Another year, and they would have bankrupted us."

"So anyone who gets in your way—" She didn't want to finish, but she did have questions. "With that first bomb. Was that just to scare Link?"

"That and to destroy the fuel cell he was working on.

You weren't supposed to be there when it went off," he told Link. "I thought I had everything worked out. I'd sent that assistant of yours on that cruise, and you were supposed to be at that dinner."

Ron shook his head. "As I said, you're just as unpredictable as your mother. I'd been worried enough that you were going to mess up everything by not letting your assistant go on the cruise. I never expected you to stop by the lab after the award dinner."

"The bomb was in Diane's briefcase," Annie said. "Were you going to blame this on her?"

"If necessary."

"Is that why you had her making those calls? So it would look like she was involved?"

"She's so gullible, it's ridiculous." He gave Link a scathing look. "Not one of your wiser choices in assistants." Then he smiled. "But she does make a good pawn."

He said it so casually, a chill ran down Annie's spine. Only one thought gave her hope, and she also smiled. "You're going to have trouble blaming this on Diane when they match the fingerprint they found on that last bomb to you."

Link's uncle didn't react as she'd expected. His look was mildly tolerant and definitely patronizing. "You're assuming that fingerprint is mine."

Annie knew, then, how cunning Ron Sheffield was. "It's Diane's fingerprint, isn't it? But how did you know where I lived?"

He shrugged. "It's really not difficult to get information if you know how to ask. Once I knew for certain that

Link was with you, I flew back to San Francisco. The receptionist at Glencove was more than willing to give an FBI agent your address and phone number. Of course, you might have some trouble working there again after what I told them, but then, I don't think you really need to worry about that."

Annie got his message. Dead people didn't need jobs. First he would kill Link, then he would kill her. It wouldn't matter to him. Just two more people who'd gotten in his way taken care of. They'd probably end up buried under some tree in a park and no one would ever know. They hadn't told anyone they were coming to Ron's house. Detective Bronson thought they were on their way to Detroit right now. The rental truck and fuel cell in front of the house would disappear, maybe be found someday at the bottom of a lake or canyon. There would be no fingerprints, and the fingerprint Detective Bronson had would only lead to Diane. If Bronson, for any reason, suspected Link's uncle, Annie was sure Ron Sheffield would have an alibi. He'd been in Europe. How could he have sent a bomb to Annie's house? No one would be able to connect the phone calls or the delivery of that second bomb to him, and she'd bet no one at Glencove would be able to identify him. Ron Sheffield was smart and cunning, and if they were going to stop him, they would have to do it themselves.

"This is really so scary," she said, with perfect honesty. "It just— I just—" She took a step forward, gasped, and threw her head back. "I—"

Rolling her head from side to side, she staggered to the side, away from Sheffield, then made a gagging sound and dropped to the floor. Though the fall jarred her, she ignored the pain and began writhing, flailing her arms and legs, rolling her head back and forth, and making gruesome noises.

Now! she thought, hoping Link understood what she was doing. *Make your move now!*

For a moment Link didn't understand. Watching Annie fall to the floor, he wanted to go to her, help her. Then he remembered.

She'd related this scene to him in the car on the way to the doctor's. It had been in one of the mysteries she'd read. Villain had gun pointed at hero. Heroine came in, pretended she was having a seizure, and while the villain was distracted, the hero saved the day.

Well, if he was going to be a hero, he'd better do something fast.

His uncle was looking at Annie, his gun aimed halfway between them. Dropping the papers in his hand, Link rushed at Ron, knowing he only had a second, if that much, before his uncle realized what was happening. Link's right leg protested the strain when he tackled his uncle's midsection, but Link ignored it and used his forward momentum to drive Ron off balance. The gun went off, and Link could only pray that the bullet hadn't hit Annie. Grabbing for his uncle's arm, he twisted it, slamming Ron's hand against the wall. He heard a clatter when the gun hit the hardwood floor, but he didn't have time to go after it.

His uncle was fighting, struggling, and his uncle had more body weight, and Link suspected more strength. He certainly couldn't hold him down.

A fist hit his face, and he struck back with a punch of his own, but still he didn't stop his uncle from regaining his feet. Scrambling to his own feet, Link tackled him again, wrapping his legs around his uncle's legs to pull him down.

He knew the moment he hit the floor that he'd caught his right leg between his uncle and the doorjamb. His leg twisted awkwardly, his uncle's weight coming down hard on it. Link heard the snap, and the pain was instantaneous, a wave of nausea following. He fought it down and tightened his hold on his uncle's arms.

And then a shot rang out, and Annie's voice cut through his pain. "Enough!" she yelled.

His uncle went still and looked up at her. So did Link. She was holding the gun, aiming it at them, the look in her eyes a mixture of fear and anger. He scooted away from his uncle, dragging his broken leg and ignoring the pain. Pulling himself to her side, he turned back toward his uncle who lay staring up at Annie.

"Give me the gun," Link said, reaching up for it. "I'll keep it on him while you call 911."

She handed him the gun, and Link knew it was over. All he had to do was keep from passing out until the police arrived.

Annie paced the hotel room, constantly looking at her watch. Link had said he would know by noon. It was after one o'clock. If he thought she was going to stay here, waiting for him to remember her—

She heard a click at the door and knew someone,

hopefully Link, had slipped in the magnetized key card. The knob turned, and the door opened.

"Well?" she asked the moment she saw him.

His grin ran from ear to ear. Leaning on his crutches, he raised a fist in a silent shout.

"You did it." She could hardly believe it. The wait was over. "They accepted your fuel cell?"

He swung himself over to where she stood, let the crutches fall onto the bed, and balancing himself on his left leg, wrapped his arms around her. "Not only did they accept it, they thought it was fantastic."

He kissed her. "They thought *I* was fantastic." He kissed her again. "Did you know I'm a genius?"

"So I've heard."

Annie snuggled against him. His embrace felt so good, so right. It was over. The waiting. The terror. Everything. In her joy, though, there was remorse.

"Now what?" she asked.

"I work with their designers, talk to their lawyers. They want it outright, which is fine with me. I accomplished what I set out to accomplish."

"The best hydrogen fuel cell around. So now, on to bigger and better things?"

"You know me," he said. "Always trying to come up with that perfect mousetrap."

"I know you." And to know him was to love him. She blinked away tears.

"You don't seem happy." He held her back slightly, looking at her face, then frowned, lifting a hand to catch a tear she hadn't stopped. "What's the matter? I thought you'd be excited."

"I am excited." She forced a smile. "I'm just . . . I don't know. Maybe it's letdown. Everything is over now. We know who was trying to kill you. You know what happened to your mother, that she didn't desert you, and what happened to your brother and father. You know your fuel cell is the best. It's . . . it's like reading a book and coming to the end, only you don't want it to end."

His frown deepened. "You cry at the end of books?"

"Sometimes."

"Weird." He shook his head, then grinned. "Well, this story hasn't ended." Sitting on the bed, he pulled her down with him. "Now it's on to our beautiful heroine. Will Annie Marsden become a doctor? A mystery writer? Or both?"

"Yeah right." She laughed. "I think you're getting into the fantasy realm now."

"Only if we don't get your applications in right away."

"What applications?"

"For medical school, of course." He looked at her as if she were slow-witted. "I have no idea how long the process takes, or where the best schools are. I want you to know, however, if we need to relocate, that's fine with me. One thing about being an inventor, location isn't of prime importance."

"If *we* need to relocate?" She was afraid to hope what that might mean. "Link, are you saying—?" She made a joining motion with her hand. "You? Me?"

He shrugged. "I figured, if you wanted to hang around for a while, I could probably tolerate you. I've gotten kind of used to you." He grinned. "You're not bad-looking, and you've got a nice voice. Not too loud. And you don't fuss, at least not too much."

She wasn't sure if she wanted to laugh or give him a poke. "If it's my looks and my voice you like, I'll give you a picture and a tape recording."

"Well, I kind of like other things about you too." He smiled wickedly. "Besides, you don't have a house to go back to, and there's plenty of room at my place. Course, you'll probably take off the first argument we have."

"Do you really believe that?"

"No." He cupped her face and looked deep into her eyes. "One thing I've learned about you, Annie Marsden, is you stick around. Heck, I can't get rid of you. I might as well marry you."

She'd figured he was asking her to move in with him. She hadn't realized he was proposing marriage. "You want to marry me?"

"What did you think we were talking about?"

"I thought we were talking about living together, about—" She wasn't sure what she'd thought. "You really want to marry me?"

"Hey, if you're afraid I'm going to hop from bed to bed the way your ex did, forget it. I don't do things like that."

Annie knew he wouldn't. She also knew he would get totally involved with any project he was working on and would forget her for hours, maybe even days. And he would be gruff and grumbly when things didn't go as he wanted, and that he wasn't going to change. There was only one thing she didn't know. "Do you love me?"

He frowned again. "Do I love you? Of course I love you."

"Of course," she repeated, and grinned. "Well, if it matters, I love you too."

"Of course." He smiled and drew her close. Near her ear, he whispered, "It matters."

Dan Zura sat next to Link, just as he'd stood next to him five years earlier when Annie and Link had said their vows. Today he was with Link to celebrate Annie's graduation. Just on the other side of Dan were Annie's parents and brother. Three other family members were missing.

Ron Sheffield would hear about Annie's graduation the next time Link visited him. In spite of everything that had happened, Link did go to the prison once a month. Annie went as well when she could, though medical school and having a baby had kept her pretty busy the last five years.

Annie's sister had stayed back at the house to baby-sit. As was proper, her father had said. Link hadn't argued. He'd found arguing with Annie's father was a no-win situation.

Joe Marsden had made it clear from the start that he didn't think his daughter had the brains to be a doctor. Even now, Link could hear him mumbling that he couldn't believe it, that the school must have lowered its standards to meet those affirmative action quotas and that women doctors weren't any good anyway. Annie's mother said nothing, she simply smiled.

Link knew Annie would be a great doctor. Graduating

eighth in her class was proof enough that the school hadn't lowered its standards to admit her, and Link had a feeling Annie would have done even better if she hadn't had the little interruption of giving birth to their daughter. Then again, both of them felt Rachel Sheffield was worth the drop of a few rankings. And if he wasn't mistaken, as grumbly as Annie had been lately, she was going to have an interruption in her internship program too. He'd have to get back to work on that automatic baby-soother he'd started when Rachel was an infant. If it worked, maybe he'd even market it. The toy he'd made for Annie's cat was selling well.

"Dr. Annie Sheffield," the announcer called, and Link jumped to his feet, hooting loudly and waving his arms in the air as Annie started across the stage to accept her degree.

She glanced his way, wrinkled her nose, then smiled and gave two thumbs-up.

THE EDITORS' CORNER

Think about it. How would you react if love suddenly came up and bit you? Would you be ready to accept it into your life? Well, in the four LOVE-SWEPTs we have in store for you this month, each hero and heroine has to face those questions. Love takes them by surprise, and these characters, in true-to-life form, all deal with it in different fashions. We hope you enjoy reading how they handle that thing called love!

The ever-popular Fayrene Preston continues her Damaron Mark series with **THE DAMARON MARK: THE MAGIC MAN**, LOVESWEPT #878. Wyatt Damaron is sure he's dreaming. Even so, he can't resist following the lovely woman in period dress beckoning to him from the mist. As the mist recedes, Wyatt realizes that his sweet-talking sprite is flesh-and-blood contemporary Annie Logan. Wyatt is most definitely a man unlike any Annie has been used to, but something about the danger and passion lurking in his eyes has her thinking more than twice about him. He is a spellbinding sorcerer who promises to dazzle and amaze her, and in that he doesn't fail. He'd vowed to protect Annie from all that threatens to keep them apart, but will Annie trust him long enough to let him succeed? Fayrene doesn't disappoint in this sizzling novel that powerfully explores the fate of kindred spirits whose destinies are forever entwined.

Cheryln Biggs takes you on a high-speed chase through Louisiana low country in **HIDDEN TREASURE**, LOVESWEPT #879. Slade Morgan and Chelsea Reynolds are both out to recover a priceless pair of stolen antique perfume bottles—but for different reasons. For Slade it's a job he's been hired to do, for Chelsea it's a chance to prove she can accomplish more for her company in the field than behind a desk. A dangerous game of cat and mouse ensues, making for close quarters and breathless adventure. You'll be glad you came along for the ride as one reckless rebel of a hero meets his match in an unlikely damsel in distress.

Author Catherine Mulvany returns at her humorous best with her second LOVESWEPT, #880. Mallory Scott has always had trouble trusting men. Wouldn't you be **MAN SHY** if your boyfriend of eleven years left you for your own sister? Now Mallory has to find a date for the happy couple's upcoming nuptials. But he can't be just any man, he has to be one hunk of a guy. Enter Brody Hunter. Sexy mouth, silver gray eyes, tousled chocolate brown hair—in short, drop-dead gorgeous. More than enough man to ward off the pitying looks sure to be given her at the wedding. Brody can't understand why the beautiful Mallory has to hunt for an escort, but who is he to argue with good fortune? Will the potent attraction they feel be strong enough to convince Mallory to drop the carefully planned game of let's pretend? Let Catherine Mulvany show you in this outrageous romp of a romance!

Please welcome newcomer Caragh O'Brien and her stunningly sensual debut, **MASTER TOUCH**, LOVESWEPT #881. When worldly art dealer Milo Dansforth requests art restorer Therese Carroll's services, she's not sure she wants the hassle. She's quite satisfied with her quiet existence. But Milo is counting on Therese's loyalty to her father to ensure that she'll take on the job—she's the only one with the expertise to do the restoration on his priceless portrait. In a makeshift art conservatory set up in a Boston studio, Therese races the clock to finish the project and discover the secrets that lay beneath the surface of both the painting and its mysterious owner. Milo tantalizes Therese with his every touch, and suddenly the painting is not the only thing these two lovers have in common. Caragh O'Brien's talent shines bright in this tapestry of tender emotion and breath-stealing mystique. Look for more from Caragh in the near future!

Happy reading!

With warmest wishes,

Susann Brailey

Joy Abella

Susann Brailey
Senior Editor

Joy Abella
Administrative Editor